BLOOPER FREAK

The Worst Detective Ever, Book 5

CHRISTY BARRITT

River Heights

 Created with Vellum

While You Were Sweeping

The Worst Detective Ever
    #1 Ready to Fumble
    #2 Reign of Error
    #3 Safety in Blunders
    #4 Join the Flub
    #5 Blooper Freak
    #6 Flaw Abiding Citizen (coming in November)

Holly Anna Paladin Mysteries:
    #1 Random Acts of Murder
    #2 Random Acts of Deceit
    #3 Random Acts of Malice
    #3.5 Random Acts of Scrooge
    #4 Random Acts of Greed
    #5 Random Acts of Fraud

Carolina Moon Series:
    Home Before Dark
    Gone By Dark
    Wait Until Dark
    Light the Dark
    Taken by Dark

Suburban Sleuth Mysteries:
    #1 Death of the Couch Potato's Wife

The Sierra Files:
  #1 Pounced
  #2 Hunted
  #2.5 Pranced (a Christmas novella)
  #3 Rattled
  #4 Caged (coming soon)

The Gabby St. Claire Diaries (a Tween Mystery series):
  #1 The Curtain Call Caper
  #2 The Disappearing Dog Dilemma
  #3 The Bungled Bike Burglaries

Standalone Romantic-Suspense:
  Keeping Guard
  The Last Target
  Race Against Time
  Ricochet
  Key Witness
  Lifeline
  High-Stakes Holiday Reunion
  Desperate Measures
  Hidden Agenda
  Mountain Hideaway
  Dark Harbor
  Shadow of Suspicion
  The Baby Assignment (coming January 2018)

Cape Thomas Series:
  Dubiosity

Disillusioned
Distorted

Standalone Romantic Mystery:
The Good Girl

Suspense:
Imperfect
The Wrecking

Nonfiction:
Changed: True Stories of Finding God through Christian Music

The Novel in Me: The Beginner's Guide to Writing and Publishing a Novel

Season 1, Episode 5

The case of real life being nothing like TV. Like, at all.
Nada. None. Zero.

Chapter One

———————

"SO THEN I GOT ALL CONFUSED." My hands flew in the air as I tried to explain what had happened. After all, why speak with only your lips when you could use your whole body? "He said, 'tennis bracelet,' and my mind went blank. Like, stressed blank, which is totally different than regular blank. I'm sure you've never had that happen."

Jackson Sullivan—the gorgeous man I'd met for breakfast—never got flustered. Even now he casually leaned back and listened to my every word with a rock-solid demeanor that fascinated me.

"I mean, people think that because I'm an actress that I'm quick on my feet, but if you put me on the spot, I freeze," I continued.

"I've seen that a few times." Jackson took another sip of coffee.

Hollywood didn't always get it right, but the whole cop in a donut shop thing? Yeah, it was so happening right now. Two of Jackson's colleagues had come in since we'd arrived twenty minutes ago. And, just to set the record straight, coming here had been Jackson's idea, not mine.

After all, I was on a raw food diet. Unless I wasn't. Like now.

"So I looked at Steve Harvey, and I was totally like, 'Tennis bracelet? But I don't play sports.'"

Jackson threw his head back in laughter. "Oh, Joey, you didn't?"

My cheeks heated just thinking about it. "Oh, I did. He thought I was joking, so I tried to play it off." I did a face palm as dread pooled in my stomach. "Just wait until it airs next week. I'll be the laughingstock of the country."

I'd just done a guest spot on a new TV game show called *Celebrity Truth or Dare*. I'd totally blown it on question number five though. "My only comfort is in knowing that Mel B—of Spice Girls and *America's Got Talent* fame—was on my team. I'm hoping they'll edit my part out and focus on her off-the-chain antics instead."

I sighed and picked up my donut. Jackson was on duty, and I was tagging along like the Donkey following Shrek. Only I was a tweeting Donkey with ulterior motives.

"How's your donut?" he asked. "Speaking of which, didn't Raven Remington like donuts?"

"She did. And this is delicious. The donuts on the set were always stale by the time I ate them. Sometimes we had to do ten or twelve takes in one scene. To say I was sick of donuts would be an understatement."

"That's a lot of takes . . . and donuts."

"For real. And you wonder why I'm always on a diet? I'm only thankful that it wasn't ice cream. TV ice cream is the worst. You know what they use for ice cream, don't you?"

"I can't say I've ever paid attention."

"It's mashed potatoes."

He made a face. "Really?"

"Really. All those cute little scenes with characters outside on a hot day eating their ice box treats? They're really licking mashed potatoes on a cone."

He made another face complete with downturned lips and squinty eyes. "I'll never view those scenes the same again."

"You can thank me later for pulling back the veil for you."

His phone rang, and he put it to his ear, mumbled a few things, and then his whole demeanor changed, morphing from relaxed to professional.

He ended the call and stood. "We have to go."

The tone of his voice made it clear that this wasn't *just* a call; this was a big deal. I just wasn't sure what kind of big deal. Was it a big deal like Meryl Streep getting nearly twenty Oscar nods? Or was it more like being nominated for Harvard's Hasty Pudding award?

I stood also, thankful I could finally walk without crutches. I'd been on them for two weeks after I'd stepped on some broken glass and sprained my ankle. By no means had I mastered the devices during that time.

"A break-in?" I followed Jackson toward the door, grabbing the last bite of my maple and bacon donut. I was now a convert. Bacon truly *was* good on everything.

"Nope." He tossed his remaining coffee and his glaze-crusted napkin into the trash can.

I hurried behind him. "Traffic accident?"

"Not this time."

"An alien abduction?"

That caused him to pause for half a step and look at me. "Really?"

I shrugged innocently. "Well, I'm running out of ideas."

He shifted, and our gazes met. "If you must know, we've got a body."

My pulse spiked, almost as if he'd said I'd been offered the role of a lifetime in a romantic saga that ended with a wash of Nicholas Sparks-worthy tears. "A body?"

Dead bodies weren't all that common in the resort area of Nags Head, North Carolina. Well, they weren't until I came to town five months ago. But this time, I was nowhere near whatever had happened. My life had been surprisingly calm the last three weeks.

Once outside, I climbed into Jackson's police-issued sedan. I wanted to pepper him with questions, but I didn't have the chance. No sooner had I closed and locked my door than Jackson was back on his phone communicating with other officers on the scene.

They used terms I had trouble translating. Ten thirty-five. Ten forty. Eight six seven five three oh nine.

Wait.

I didn't think he'd used that last number, but all the numerals were now jumbled together in my head.

All I could do was sit there and listen—two things I wasn't great at doing.

A few minutes later, we pulled to a stop in the driveway of an oceanside McMansion complete with weathered cedar shingles and cheerful yellow hurricane shutters. I followed Jackson over the sand dune, struggling to keep up with him.

"You have to stay on the other side of the police line," he reminded me.

"Of course."

"And try not to talk to anyone about what's going on."

"I would never."

"And don't take pictures or tweet anything."

I acted offended. "Oh ye of little faith."

Basically, I was there to observe. And like a good little girl, that was what I'd do. Of course.

I mean, far be it for me to ever stick my nose where it didn't belong. Like, ever.

I was much more mellow than that.

And the *Star Wars* franchise was dying, Steven Spielberg would never have another hit, and Hollywood actors were forfeiting pay for the greater good.

Yeah, right.

As soon as we crossed the sand dune, I paused and sucked in a breath. I knew the shoreline had been eroding with the recent storms, but I hadn't expected this. The sand beneath the McMansion had been washed away. The pilings there, which were normally visible, were now totally exposed—all the way down to the very bottom, like dinosaur bones at a dig site.

But immediately my attention shifted from the pilings to what was beneath the structure.

Yellow crime-scene tape sectioned off the area. For good reason. A hand, arm, and leg protruded from the sandy embankment.

By all appearances, this person had been buried

there, and during last night's thunderstorm, the ocean had washed away the sand concealing the body.

I looked closer. The hand told me the victim was Caucasian. Based on the hair there, he was a man—or a very hairy woman. I was going to go with a man.

I also saw a gold watch that looked expensive. The fact that it hadn't been stolen told me this wasn't a robbery.

The skin was still intact and only slightly discolored, which probably meant the body was fresh and this crime was recent.

"Stay here," Jackson reminded me.

I nodded obediently. My alter ego, Raven Remington, would never listen to orders at a crime scene. But I wasn't Raven Remington, as I constantly had to remind people. Apparently, I needed to remind *myself* of that also.

Raven was the ace detective I'd played on my hit TV show. Unfortunately, the two of us were nothing alike. Everything I'd ever learned about crime fighting I'd learned from her. And Jackson.

Jackson slipped under the police tape to check out the scene.

I waited patiently. But the truth was that real police work was so boring, nothing like what happened on TV.

There were so many details and protocols to attend to in real life. And you know what else? DNA never came back in a day. Fingerprints could take hours—if not longer. Unglamorous paperwork consumed much of a cop's time. If this was *CSI*, this crime would already be solved, the whole gang would be going out for drinks together, and there would have been six commercial breaks in between.

I lingered for what felt like hours. Hours.

At first I stood at the police line.

Then I sat in the sand.

I built a sandcastle with a little seven-year-old girl visiting from New York.

I constructed a tower of broken shells with a two-year-old.

I reenacted the *Chariots of Fire* running scene with a group of lifeguards in training. We even sang the wordless music as we did so.

Then I sat back in the sand and watched the beautiful waves wash ashore. They were big today—red flags were flying on the lifeguard stands, warning everyone against going in the water.

I watched dolphins frolicking in the massive waves.

Did I mention how long actual police work took? Hours. Hours and hours.

Then I glanced at my watch. It had only been forty minutes since I got here. What? That couldn't be right.

I had to do something else to occupy my mind here.

So I thought back over the past several weeks and all the changes that had happened.

I'd moved out of my oceanside cottage because the owner wanted top dollar for the premium summer months. I was now staying in a condo on the sound—a condo that just happened to be owned by Winston Corbina, a man I suspected of being involved with my dad's disappearance.

Please, no one accuse of me of not thinking ahead. At least, in this case. Career-wise, fashion-wise, and diet-wise were all up for grabs though.

My last movie was such a success that the IRS was able to take all my money and clear me of my debt to them. That meant I didn't have to work at Beach Combers, a salon, anymore. I was now officially on emergency backup, but I did try to stop by once a week or so to help Dizzy and get my social fix with her and her Hot Chick friends.

My ex, Eric, appeared to be gone from my life permanently. Our debt no longer connected us, and I was pretty certain Jackson had scared him away from ever coming around me again. Win-win!

My manager, Rutherford, had been humbled enough during a recent life-threatening snafu that it saved our relationship. For now, I was still working with him. I still might fire him eventually. I just had to decide about my future first.

Yep, that about summed it up.

After another hour had passed—okay, it had been only five minutes—I made my way over to the police line again and watched the scene playing out in front of me.

Jackson took a brush and began to wipe away the sand near the body. Eventually a face emerged.

I sucked in a breath.

I recognized that face.

It looked like my streak of being noninvolved in crimes was coming to an abrupt and unfortunate end.

Chapter Two

It was Morty Savage.

Morty worked at a shady restaurant/bar called Willie Wahoo's and was a good friend of Billy Corbina.

Billy was trouble, and I'd always suspected that he had something to do with my father's disappearance— just like his father, Winston Corbina. I just hadn't expected this . . . hadn't expected one of his friends to be . . . dead.

For that matter, I'd seen Morty only a few days ago. I hated Willie Wahoo's, but I loved trying to figure out what happened to my father. That required at least observing a bit of the area's underworld. I considered Willie Wahoo's part of that underworld. Only this underworld didn't include Kate Beckinsale or any special effects. No, it was all body odor and rowdy drunks.

I desperately wanted more information about Morty's death.

But from my little place behind the police line, there was no information to be found.

Which stunk.

I stared at the officers as they worked. Mostly I stared at Jackson, who looked especially nice with his sleeves rolled up. He was in serious work mode—all in charge and in control. I could watch him like that all day.

A crowd gathered. A couple of people asked for my autograph. Some surfers paused long enough to gawk.

Another hour later—okay, only ten minutes—I sensed someone mosey up beside me, and glanced over. A stout, middle-aged man who reminded me of Kevin James from *Mall Cop* and *The King of Queens* stood there. He wore a thick gold chain around his neck, and his stained white T-shirt and exercise shorts led me to believe he just woke up.

"The wifey told me to come check things out." He glanced at the home beside the grave-front mansion and waved at the woman standing on the balcony. She scowled and went back inside. "She's a little cranky this morning. It's not even nine o'clock. You should be able to sleep in until noon on vacation. I should ask for a discount."

"Bummer."

He did a double take. "Do I know you? You look familiar."

I decided to forgo sharing the fact that I was an actress. "I don't think we've ever met. Maybe I just have one of those faces."

He shrugged, accepting my answer, and turned back to the crime scene. "What happened?"

"Dead body." Grief stretched through my voice. In order to honor life, you had to honor death.

Raven Remington had once said that, but it had always stuck with me.

His eyes widened. "Really? I was out here last night, taking a walk to blow off steam after my wife and I had a fight. I saw two guys arguing. I couldn't figure out what they were arguing about, but it looked heated. I figured I should mind my own business."

"Really?" Had this man witnessed something connected to this death? That was what it sounded like.

I definitely needed to tell Jackson—right after I asked a few more questions. I mean, Jackson was busy right now, so I shouldn't interrupt him until I had all the facts.

"Do you remember anything about the guys you saw?" I asked, the morning sun already warm on my back.

The man shrugged. "Not much. I mean, it was dark, and I was trying not to stare."

"So you didn't notice anything specific?" I tried to reframe my original question—a technique I'd learned from Jackson.

He let out a breath. "Well, I guess I did. One of them had one of those man-bun things, and he was wearing a bright-orange tank top."

"Okay . . ." That was a start. Lots of guys my age liked doing the man-bun thing. Unfortunately. And bright-orange tank tops? Anyone could have one.

Despite my rationalization, something nagged at the back of my mind. I tried to ignore it.

"And—this could be unrelated—but when I went back up to my house, I stepped onto the deck. I saw one of the guys leaving. He climbed into one of those camper-van things."

My heart raced a couple of beats.

"A camper van?" I repeated as reality tried to settle on me.

"That's right."

I didn't want to face the truth, but the person he'd just described fit that of my friend Zane Oakley to a T.

"Jackson, Zane wouldn't have done this."

I'd called him over to the police line and shared what I'd heard. He'd talked to Kevin James and gotten his statement before turning back to me. I could read his thoughts before he spoke a word.

"He couldn't have," I reiterated.

Jackson's gaze darkened at my words. I knew exactly what he was thinking. He was thinking that Zane *totally* could have done this.

It wasn't that Zane was a bad guy. It was just that he had a history of making bad choices. And drug addiction. And wearing unfortunate man buns.

"We need to find him," Jackson said.

I quickly reviewed everything I knew, and I stopped at one major sticking point that would prove once and for all that Zane was innocent. "He's down in Florida."

Jackson frowned. "Would you mind calling him? Please, Joey."

"I thought I needed to stay out of this." I really liked to be in the middle of things only by my own volition. Right now, I was so uncomfortable that even my discomfort was uncomfortable. I should never have brought this up.

"Joey . . ." I heard the urgency in his voice.

I wiped my forehead as the sun glared down at me. It was hot. Had I mentioned that yet? And I was already hungry. Apparently, maple bacon donuts didn't really fill you up. And I didn't want to call Zane while under Jackson's watchful gaze.

I felt like I was in my own version of *Speed*—I'd set something in motion, and now I couldn't stop it. And even if I did stop it, it would end with an explosion.

"Okay, okay." I raised my hands, pushing images of Sandra Bullock and bus crashes out of my head. "I'll call him. But what do I say?"

"Ask him where he is."

I swallowed hard, feeling a rush of anxiety. "I can't lie to him, Jackson."

He squeezed my arm, probably trying to calm me down. "I'm not asking you to lie. I'm asking you to find out where he is."

Still, tension snaked up my spine as I pulled my phone out. I hesitated only another minute before dialing Zane's number. I comforted myself by thinking he wouldn't answer. And that he was in Florida. This was all one big, bad mistake.

I hadn't called him since he left. He'd said he was leaving so he could put distance between himself and some bad influences in the area. I'd figured he'd call me when he was back. We were tight like that.

To my surprise, Zane answered on the first ring. "Joey?"

My throat clutched, and I turned away from Jackson. It was the closest I could get to privacy. "Zane? Where are you?"

"Joey . . ." A frantic undertone edged his voice,

making me think I'd caught him at a bad time—a bad time in Florida. "It's a long story."

I didn't like how this conversation was starting. "Where are you?"

"I'm staying with my friend down in Waves."

Okay, I was 0 for 2. Zane had answered, *and* he was in town. My odds weren't looking good, but Zane's were looking even worse.

"When did you get back to this area? I can't believe you didn't call me." I had to throw that in there.

I glanced over my shoulder long enough to see Jackson give me a look that clearly said, *Stay focused.*

"It's a long story," he muttered.

"Where are you exactly, Zane?" I asked. "Where in Waves?"

"I'm staying with Abe."

Abe? He seemed like an unfortunate choice as a roommate, however temporary. I got bad vibes from the guy.

Jackson mouthed something to me. I finally interpreted it and said, "Stay there, Zane."

"Why?" His voice cracked. "Why would I stay here? What's going on, Joey?"

I glanced at Jackson, pondering how much to say. Jackson motioned for me to keep going.

"Just stay there," I finally said. "Please."

Chapter Three

JACKSON HAD CALLED the Dare County Sheriff's Department to pick up Zane, probably because Hatteras Island—where the village of Waves was located—was out of his jurisdiction.

An hour and twenty-two minutes later, Zane was at the Nags Head Police Station and Jackson was questioning him. I wasn't in the room. Instead, I stayed outside in the hallway, pacing and waiting. I hoped and prayed that Zane had a great explanation for this.

Certainly he did. I mean, of *course* he did. No doubt. He should be *Presumed Innocent* all the way right now. Except not like the movie. Because wasn't the innocent guy actually guilty? Or maybe not. It didn't matter right now.

What mattered right now was that Zane wasn't capable of murder. He was many things, but a killer wasn't one of them.

It would be like Bambi becoming a hunter instead of a victim. The universe would tilt and shift because it knew something wasn't right. I just needed to wait this out, and certainly I would learn that this was all a big, huge misunderstanding.

Finally, Jackson stepped out of the room, his expression as dark and stormy as the beginning of a really turbulent movie—like *Twister*.

I rushed toward him, trying to gauge how tight lipped he would be. It was no use—I couldn't get a good read on him. I did know one thing: Jackson was going to do the right thing, and I wouldn't change his mind. Not that I'd want to or anything. Doing the right thing was the right thing.

"Well?" I pressed my lips together.

He rubbed his jaw, his gaze burdened and troubled. "It doesn't look good, Joey."

I touched his arm and then remembered that we were supposed to be professional. I pulled away as if I'd touched fire and tried to compose myself. "Let me talk to Zane. Please."

Jackson studied me a minute, his green eyes full of discernment and wisdom that I'd come to value. "If you do, we'll be listening to every word you say."

I raised my chin, not one to be deterred. And people listened to every word I said all the time. Especially reporters when I was saying something stupid. So this wouldn't be anything new for me.

"That's okay," I said. "I don't have anything to hide."

He raised an eyebrow. "You weren't the one I was worried about."

"He didn't do this, Jackson. I know Zane."

Jackson didn't react—either agree or disagree. He only said, "Go talk to him yourself."

I didn't like the way that sounded. Despite that, I

nodded, drew in a deep breath, and stepped inside the bland, sterile interrogation room. I felt a bit like the one who was being accused.

The lights were dim. Was one of the fluorescents buzzing? Was that some kind of mind-game tactic?

I forgot all that when I saw Zane.

The Zane I saw sitting there wasn't the carefree Zane I knew. His eyes were bloodshot, his shoulders slumped, and his smile had disappeared like that man's psycho wife in *Gone Girl*. My stomach clenched as I read between the lines: he was devastated.

I slid into the plastic seat across from him, some part of me instinctively mimicking his body language and hunching also.

He'd barely looked at me when I entered, so I reached across the table and touched his hands, trying to break through to him. He hardly flinched.

"Zane, what's going on?" My voice cracked.

Finally, he raised his head. As he did, he pulled his hands back. Was he rejecting me? Distancing himself? I wasn't sure.

"I didn't do this, Joey." His voice sounded hoarse and scratchy.

Unfortunately, even though I wished I could just leave it at that—that I could just take him at his word—I couldn't. I had some hard questions to ask. Questions that wouldn't help him find his lost Bob Ross Zen.

I licked my lips. "I heard you were seen with Morty right before he died. Tell me that's not true."

He drew his haggard gaze back up to mine. "Morty asked me to meet with him on the beach. But he was alive when I left him."

I swallowed hard. That wasn't what I'd wanted to

hear. "Can you start from the beginning? I didn't even think you were back in town."

Yes, for some reason, that fact was bothering me entirely too much. It was a small deceit. But if a person lied about one thing, I was inclined to believe he would lie about anything. My dad had taught me that.

I supposed Zane had no obligation to contact me, so maybe it wasn't exactly a lie of omission, even if it felt like one.

He rubbed a hand through his hair, and his gaze dropped. "I just wanted to slip back into the area and stay low for a while until I got my footing."

What did that mean? I seriously had no idea. "I can't believe you didn't even tell me. I'd like to think I help you keep your footing."

I wanted to defend him, but the fact that he was hiding things from me greatly diminished that desire.

His eyes met mine. "You do help me find my footing, Joey. Believe me—you do. It's just complicated."

"I hate when people say that." However, I said it all the time. Like, *all* the time. But that was aside from the point. "Can you tell me what happened?"

Zane drew in a long, deep breath, as if he was gathering his thoughts and needed all of the energy he could muster. "Morty called me last night around midnight. He asked me to meet him at the beach."

"Okay." This was a good start.

"When I met him there, he was acting crazy. He asked me to deliver a package to someone."

The good start went bad. When it came to crime, any kind of package was never good. No, packages only spelled trouble. I'd learned that from Raven also.

I swallowed hard. "What kind of package?"

"I'm not sure. I didn't ask. I didn't want anything to do with it."

So he knew packages were bad too. He should get some credit for that. But I still had more questions. "Why didn't you want anything to do with it?"

Finally, his gaze met mine. "Basically, it's like this. Morty and his girlfriend, Bianca, just broke up. I figured it was some of her stuff. I didn't want to get in the middle of it. That woman is crazy."

"Why did you think it was her stuff? Did he ask you to give it to her or someone else?"

"No, he didn't specifically say it was hers. But Morty had been so distraught since Bianca left him. I could just feel that this was going to be trouble. Morty has always been trouble." Zane crossed his arms and averted his gaze again. "When I left him, he was alive and he still had his package."

I remembered what Kevin James had told me about a heated conversation. "But you argued first?"

"We did. Morty was adamant that I help him."

"And you were adamant that you wouldn't," I finished.

"Exactly. But I had no reason to kill him."

The door opened, and Jackson came in. His expression had morphed from a Lifetime-movie type of dark and stormy to a Stephen King–worthy one.

Dear me. This wasn't good.

He held up a bag and turned to Zane. "You recognize this?"

I stared through the plastic. There was a gun inside. A handgun, I thought. A Glock.

Zane hated guns. He'd emphasized that point when

I took him to a gun range a few weeks ago. He almost hadn't gone.

Zane remained quiet, staring a hole into the weapon.

"This was the gun used to kill Morty," Jackson said. "Your prints are on it."

Chapter Four

"I would never shoot someone!" Sweat sprinkled Zane's forehead, and his hands shook. "You've got to believe me."

"How about this?" Jackson slapped a picture on the table. "Have you seen this?"

I peered over his shoulder and saw a photo of a package wrapped in brown paper. It appeared to be the size of a brick. There was no way that could be the package Zane had seen last night.

Zane stared at the photo, and recognition flared to life in his gaze. "That's the package Morty tried to give me last night. I didn't take it."

Or maybe that *was* the package. Mental sigh.

"It was in the house where you're staying."

Zane raised his hands. "Well, I didn't put it there. And how did you get a warrant so fast?"

"We didn't need one. Your friend let us in."

Zane's bottom lip dropped, but then he clamped his mouth shut. He was mad at Abe for letting the police into his room, I realized.

"Do you know what was inside this package?" Jackson continued.

I really wished they would stop using that word.

Zane's jaw flexed. "Notes from Morty's ex-girlfriend and a straw from a drink they shared on their first date?"

"A brick of cocaine."

Zane's eyes widened. My eyes widened. Jackson's eyes, on the other hand, narrowed with a new intensity.

"I promise—I didn't take the package, I didn't know what was inside, and I have no idea how it ended up at my place."

Zane's voice climbed higher. No doubt he was realizing how this looked. It wasn't good.

"I'm sorry, Zane," Jackson continued. "The murder weapon has your prints on it, you were last seen with the victim, and this was found in your room. We have enough evidence to get a warrant for your arrest and to charge you with the murder of Morty Savage."

"I didn't do it." Veins protruded at Zane's neck, and panic visibly raked through him.

My heart pounded out of control as I watched everything unfold. I felt helpless to do anything and uncertain if I should do anything even if I could. As much as I didn't want to believe it, all the evidence definitely made Zane look guilty.

"You have the right to remain silent." Jackson pulled out his handcuffs and stepped closer to Zane, clearly on a mission.

Zane turned toward me, desperation in his gaze. "Joey, you've got to help figure out who did this. Help clear my name. Please."

I didn't know what else to do but nod. "Of course. I'll do whatever I can."

Jackson shot me a scowl. Apparently he didn't want me doing that. But how could I say no? My friend needed me. And what were friends for if not to help prove you weren't a murderer?

"Considering your connection to this case, I think it would be best if you weren't working with me right now, Joey," Jackson said as he led Zane toward the door. No doubt he was going to book him, and Zane's life was going to look dramatically different for a while.

Then Jackson's words hit me, and my cheeks flushed. Ouch. Jackson was firing me? But I'd never even been hired! How rude.

At least without Jackson by my side, I could snoop freely and without obstruction.

If only I could do that without harming myself.

Baby steps.

Inwardly, I felt incredibly unsettled at the silent friction I felt between Jackson and me though.

I slipped out of the room while Jackson read Zane his rights.

If I stayed much longer, Jackson would read me something also—the riot act.

And nobody had time for that.

As I left the police station and walked toward my car, I felt a bit dejected. I wasn't sure why. I supposed it was that Jackson and I were usually on the same side. Unless I was sticking my nose where it didn't belong. And I supposed this situation counted for that.

So that still didn't explain my gloomy feelings.

I shouldn't be walking to my car alone right now. I should be with Jackson.

But a good friend had been accused of murder by another good friend, so I supposed that did put me between a rock and a hard place. I never realized what a lonely position that was to be in until now.

The good news was that it was possible to climb out with just a little bit of effort.

And that was exactly what I planned on doing right now.

I shoved my shoulders back and slipped my aviator sunglasses on. Dejected or not, I had to prove that Zane wasn't behind this.

Except . . . what if he was? I nearly stumbled on a pebble as the thought crossed my mind.

This was all too confusing. Why couldn't it be like it was in the movies, where everything seemed so cut and dry?

Real life was never quite that simple. Everything couldn't be wrapped up in 130 minutes with all your questions answered and every relationship coming into absolute and complete clarity. Real life was much more winding and twisty with no time limits on your challenges and obstacles.

I continued toward my car. It was June, and it was hot here on the Outer Banks of North Carolina. Not only was it hot, but it was humid. Once you stepped past the dunes toward the ocean, a nice offshore breeze cooled you off—on most days, at least.

But right here in the middle of asphalt, there was no relief. Heat sizzled from the dark ground beneath me, promising to burn my feet if I dared to step on it barefoot.

I paused, and the skin on my neck crawled.

I glanced around, looking for the source of my unease. Multiple cars and police cruisers were in the lot. A mailman passed and waved on a side street to my left. Some seagulls swooped overhead, threatening to dive-bomb me if I didn't drop some food.

My gaze stopped at a man in the distance. He stood on the sidewalk near the highway, stretching his quad muscle and sporting running gear.

Even though he was wearing sunglasses, I could tell he was staring at me.

As soon as our gazes met, he dropped his leg from stretching position and jogged away.

Was that . . .

I squinted and shook my head.

It almost looked like Leonard Shepherd, a man who'd stalked me in California. I'd gotten a restraining order against him, and I thought we were done. But he'd shown up here a few months ago, saved my life, and then disappeared again.

Certainly that wasn't him.

But the two men had such similar features . . .

I shook my head again.

Everything was just messing with my mind.

Despite that logic, I quickly climbed into my car and locked my doors. I cranked the engine and waited for the AC to do its job. As the seconds ticked by, I tried to think everything through.

What would Raven Remington do?

She'd start by putting together a timeline. She'd question other people who'd been around Zane. Maybe try to put together Morty Savage's final hours. She'd follow one lead and decide it was either worthwhile or not, and then she would proceed.

That was what I'd do as well.

I let the cool air wash over me. So where did I start?

I'd go to Abe's place, where Zane had been staying. Where that package of cocaine had been found. With any luck, Abe would be home, and he'd have some insight. A friend of Zane's would be a friend of mine also. Right?

I would do this with or without Jackson.

It wasn't hard to figure out where Abe lived—it just took a quick Google search. To say I had a lot of reservations about the man would be an understatement. But like any good detective, I pushed aside my fears and ignored every flaming instinct as I walked up the steps toward his front door.

Um . . . right?

This was beach country, which meant every building that anyone with good sense had constructed was up on stilts in case of tidal flooding. Somehow the height also seemed more imposing, especially when I considered all someone had to do was give me a good shove and I'd topple over a railing, plunging a story to my death—or at least a mighty good injury.

Abe was waiting at the door by the time I got to the top. The man was probably in his late forties. He was lean, athletic, tatted up, and he wore his salt-and-pepper hair back in a ponytail. Like many aging surfers, his skin was sun wrinkled.

All the moisture left my throat when I saw him.

Zane, I reminded myself. I was doing this for Zane. He'd been a good friend to me, and now I would be a good friend to him. Even if it meant talking to people who made me uncomfortable.

Like Abe.

"What brings you here?" A toothpick dangled from his mouth, and he gave off a cocky vibe.

He didn't actually open his door, but instead he spoke through the screen, his beady eyes watching my every move.

I raised my chin. "I think you know."

His eyes sparkled with some kind of sick amusement. "Where's your little friend?"

"I don't know who you're talking about." Zane? Certainly Abe realized where Zane was. He was up a creek that was quickly rising.

"The cop."

I cringed. He was talking about Jackson. The man had obviously been paying attention, and that thought left me unsettled.

"I'm not working with him right now," I said.

Take that, NHPD Blues! I'm going solo, Joey Darling style.

"So you're alone?" Something gleamed in his eyes.

Okay, solo Joey Darling style wasn't seeming all that great right now.

I took a step back, and the aged deck boards beneath my feet groaned, as if this entire structure knew that me being here was a bad idea.

I should feign an excuse and get out of here. But then how would I get any answers? It was a conundrum. A Joey Darling conundrum. I had a lot of those.

Choose wisely, little Raven.

My mentor on the TV show had always said that. His deep, gravelly voice echoed in my head now.

"Can I ask you a few questions?" I raised my shoulders, trying to look tougher than I felt.

He pushed the door open, and it let out a rowdy squeak. Even Abe's house didn't like him. It was confirmed.

"Sure, come on in."

Without the screen muting his image, I could see a sardonic smile on his face.

Oh no. I would not be ignoring my instincts on this one. "I'll stay here."

"In the heat?"

Now that he mentioned it, it *was* hot. Sweat was trickling down my forehead and my back. I hoped it didn't become unsightly. If it did, a gorilla reporter from the *National Instigator* would certainly appear and document it for the world to see.

But going inside Abe's place would be a mistake. A big one.

"I like the heat." Oh, I sounded like Raven when I used that tone. Right now that was a good thing. If he sensed my weakness, no doubt he would prey on it.

His eyes glimmered with a touch of salacious malice. "Good to know."

What did that mean? This guy was creepy. How could Zane be his friend, and what did it say about Zane that he was?

But if that was true, then what did it say about me that I was Zane's friend?

My dad had always told me we'd be judged by the company we kept.

Maybe he was onto something.

"What do you need to know, sweetheart?"

"How did that package get in Zane's room?"

"I have no idea," he said. "You'd have to ask Zane that question."

"I did." I couldn't let it go that easily. "Who's come and gone today?"

"No one." He crossed his arms, and his tattoos stared back at me. Naked women. Anchors. A compass.

I pulled my sunglasses down, in full-fledged Raven mode. Man, I'd missed acting like her more than I realized. "Well, *obviously* someone left it."

"Or maybe Zane brought the package himself, Little Miss Smarty Pants."

My mouth dropped open—both at the name and his statement. The sound of waves crashing on the shores in the distance helped calm my pulsing nerves before I did something I regretted.

"What kind of friend are you?" I finally asked.

He remained unfazed. "I'm just telling the truth."

"Well, while you're telling the truth, what's been going on with Zane? How long has he been staying here?"

"He came in four days ago."

"Did he say what was going on? Why he came back? Why he came here?"

"He said he ran into some trouble."

I was getting irritated now. Why did I have to pull details from people like a sadistic dentist pulling teeth? "What kind of trouble?"

"Just this morning he told me he thought he saw someone murdered. Not sure if it's connected or not."

My eyes widened, and I stepped back again. As I

29

did, my foot hit something, and it clattered down the stairs.

I gasped, turning to see what happened.

A crushed beer can fled from Abe—which was exactly what I wanted to do.

Had Zane seen Morty's murder? That was a game changer.

Why hadn't Zane told me that earlier?

There was obviously a lot more to this story than I assumed. The challenge would be figuring how to fill in all those small but important details.

Chapter Five

I STARED AT ABE, trying not to show my rising anxiety. He continued to stare back, still chewing on that toothpick and acting as if he didn't have a care in the world. A TV blared behind him.

Was that *Relentless* I heard?

My anxiety climbed even higher.

This man wasn't right.

"Did Zane say anything else?" I pressed, knowing I was just scratching the surface of this.

I was blowing dead grass off the sidewalk when I should be trying to get to the center of the earth. But a girl had to start somewhere. And unlike Raven Remington, I was an amateur at this.

"He didn't want to talk about it," Abe said. "He wanted to chill out and process."

I could hear Zane saying that. While drinking an Izze. And watching Bob Ross.

I suddenly missed my friend with a vengeance.

I cleared my throat, trying to choose my words wisely and not give up any information that I shouldn't.

I'd like to think that I'd learned from my past mistakes, but that was still debatable. If I had, I probably wouldn't be here right now.

"Did Zane say who he saw get killed?" His story seemed so outlandish that it really threw me for a loop.

"Nah. It happened when he was out of town." Abe stared at me, waiting for my next question, almost as if he thought this was a game.

"Out of town?" So it wasn't Morty.

I couldn't think of anything else to ask him, even though I was sure I was missing something. I had a feeling Abe knew more than he was willing to say. A wiser, more savvy detective would know how to finagle the information out of him, but I was drawing a blank.

Which made me feel like a failure.

Finally, I nodded, realizing I just needed to wrap this up and regroup. "Okay then. Good talk."

"I heard about Morty." Abe still leaned against the doorframe like he had all the time fathomable. Like he was one step ahead of me—ahead of the world, for that matter.

That kind of arrogance always set me on edge. But sooner or later, things caught up with people who were cocky like that. My ex-husband, Eric, was a case in point.

"How'd you hear about Morty?" Seriously, how had he heard? Had the police said something when they'd picked up Zane? I hadn't said anything during this conversation . . . had I?

I mentally reviewed our talk, but I didn't think I'd given anything away.

Abe smirked. "Word travels fast around here."

"I guess so." I turned to leave, suddenly uncomfortable being alone with Abe. Though there were other houses around, I felt isolated.

I probably shouldn't have come here by myself.

"Be careful out there, Joey."

Abe said it as if he knew me, and he didn't.

For some reason, that annoyed me. "Oh, I will be."

Starting with Abe. I was going to start putting him in the same category as Billy Corbina. Billy was too slick for his own good, and scaring people seemed to amuse him. Why else would he have worn a mask with my face on it and followed me?

"No, really," he said. "You don't know what you're getting yourself into."

I froze as the underlying meaning in his words swept over me. Slowly, I turned toward him, desperate to see his expression. "What does that mean? What do you know that you're not telling me?"

He straightened and leaned toward me. "I don't know nothing about this investigation. But I know Morty was involved with some rough folks."

"Rougher than you?"

"A lot rougher than me." He didn't seem offended.

I supposed that was a good thing. Except that it could mean he was proud of that fact.

Some people . . . I mentally shook my head.

"Who are these guys?" I continued. "Are they a part of the regular crowd I saw Morty with at Willie Wahoo's?"

He did a nonchalant shrug. "Maybe."

"Why won't you tell me?" Irritation burned at me.

"Because I don't want things to get back to anyone that I'm running my mouth, that's why."

Just as we finished and Abe disappeared inside, a car

pulled into the driveway. Jackson and another man—a sheriff's deputy—stepped out.

I held my breath and wondered how this would go. I walked down the steps and met Jackson with a terse nod. His partner stayed back at the car.

"I should have known," Jackson said, frowning at me.

I could feel the tension crackling between us, and I didn't like it. Not one bit. Hopefully, my sunglasses concealed the range of emotions cycling through me. Disappointment. Determination. Frustration.

"I'm just asking questions," I said.

He leaned closer and lowered his voice. "Asking questions could get you killed."

"I can't just sit back and do nothing!"

"Of course you can. You can let me do my job. And you shouldn't have talked to Abe before me. What if you tipped him off in some way?"

"How would I have tipped him off?" The idea was ridiculous.

Just then, someone darted from the back of the house, running between the homes on the street.

It was Abe.

Yeah, I'd totally tipped him off. I had yet another blooper to add to my already long list.

Go, Joey. You're the Blooper Queen.

Or maybe I should say, a Blooper Freak.

Jackson easily caught Abe and tackled him.

It was pretty impressive, especially when I considered that Abe was some kind of tri-athletic marathon runner and Spartan racer.

My admiration for Jackson was short lived, however. I watched as he handcuffed Abe and dragged him back to the police car. Instead of letting me stick around, as he normally might, Jackson barked that I should go.

Barking so wasn't nice.

And it wasn't like Jackson.

Maybe he hadn't exactly barked. He'd just been . . . authoritative. And not much like the man who'd swept me off my feet with his incredible, head-spinning kisses not too long ago.

I let out a mental sigh, realizing he was just doing his job, but I wished things didn't feel so complicated.

"Joey?" he called before I climbed in my car.

"Yes?" I asked hopefully.

He closed his door—probably so Abe wouldn't hear—and stepped closer. "I thought I'd let you know—between you and me—that Zane bought a gun two days ago."

My bottom lip dropped.

"And his hands tested positive for gunshot residue," he continued.

My lip dropped even lower.

"Maybe you don't need to investigate after all."

He wanted me off this investigation. And if the evidence continued to stack up against Zane, he might get his wish. How could I refute that?

"In other news, are you still going to Phoebe's tonight?" Jackson asked.

Phoebe's? I'd nearly forgotten my friend had invited me to a bonfire there. "Yes, I'll be there. You?"

"I'm hoping I'll be able to take a break from this

case for long enough to make it. You want to ride together?"

I smiled, some of my tension disappearing. "Definitely. I'll meet you at your place. Sound good?"

"Sounds great." He smiled in return, and for a moment, the case wasn't wedged between us like moldy cheese on a platter. "I'll see you then."

So maybe he didn't hate me after all.

And maybe there was still hope for moldy-cheese platters.

Chapter Six

JACKSON AND ABE PULLED AWAY, and I remained in my car another moment. I knew whom I needed to talk to next—I just needed to do some research first.

I pulled out my phone and found Morty Savage's Facebook page. I searched his friends for a "Bianca" but came up blank. When they'd broken up, Morty had obviously removed her from his friend list or Bianca had removed him. Instead, I had to search through some mutual friends, but I finally found the person I was looking for.

Bianca Martin looked, in her online pictures at least, like somewhat of a gypsy. Her hair was cut in a severe wedge. It was black underneath and a wicked blond on top. Her nose, eyebrow, and lip were pierced, and she seemed to have an affinity for heavy black eye makeup.

I also saw that she worked for Slick Ocean Surf Shop. Zane had an endorsement deal with them and was paid to blog and feature their products in his social media.

It was worth a shot to see if she was there today.

What else did I have to do? I would visit Morty's home, but apparently he was skipping around and living with different people right now. Zane had told me once that a lot of his friends did that in the summertime, when rental rates skyrocketed.

I started the thirty-minute drive back up to Nags Head. The trip never felt burdensome because it was along the most gorgeous byway ever. Massive sand dunes stood on one side of the road, and on the other was marshland that faded into the Pamlico Sound.

At its most narrow portion, only two hundred yards separated me from the water on either side. Surfers parked on the roadside and carried boards on their heads along paths across the dunes. Tourists took pictures. A bulldozer waited on standby to push sand off the road in case a big wind kicked up.

My thoughts continued to dwell on everything that had happened. It was unbelievable, really, and seemed like a nightmare I should wake up from. I'd like to think that things like this only happened on TV. But that obviously wasn't the case here.

My phone rang, and I saw that it was my best friend, Starla, calling. I answered on Bluetooth.

"Joey! It's so good to talk to you!"

Starla's enthusiastic voice made everything feel bright for a minute.

"It's been too long, and you've been all the talk in our circles here."

"Have I?" Did I even want to know?

"Your movie premiere there in North Carolina? Carli almost dying? Eric being outed as the loser he really is? Those pictures of you with not one but two men? Girlfriend, we have got to catch up."

"You should come out and visit me sometime."

"As soon I wrap up this movie, I would love to. You know Ryan and I broke up, right? It hasn't hit the tabloids yet, but it will."

"You always were too good for him," I said.

"Oh, Joey, you're always such a good friend."

Her words only increased my resolve to help Zane.

I hadn't been able to help my dad, but I didn't want to let someone else I loved down.

———

Eventually, I reached Nags Head, and the traffic in the area thickened considerably. I found Slick Ocean, which was a freestanding building purposefully designed to look like a shack with its fake weathered siding, pretend straw roof, and a sign with colorful arrows that pointed to various beaches and indicated how far away they were.

Waikiki: 4,945 miles.

Good to know.

I prepared myself to go inside.

I always felt that as soon as I went inside some of the hardcore surf shops, the staff sensed I wasn't a real surfer. Or that I wasn't a surfer at all. At least in the past Zane had been with me, and he was like a celebrity in some of these places.

"If it's not Joey Darling!" the guy behind the counter said when I walked in. "I recognize you from Zane's videos."

Not from my People's Choice Award or from the fact that I had the number one movie at the box office for three weeks in a row or from my hit series *Relentless*.

But that was okay. It didn't bother me—more like amused me.

"What brings you by?" The employee leaned on the counter, looking incredibly bored and like he was thrilled to have an actual customer to chat with.

He seemed so happy, and that made me think that he hadn't heard about Zane yet. If he had, wouldn't he be a little more subdued? I mean, Zane being arrested wasn't exactly great publicity for Slick Ocean.

"I'm actually looking for Bianca," I started.

"Bianca . . . is . . . not . . . here . . . yet." He added a weird pause between each word and filled the spaces with awkward head nods.

I tried to read between the lines—or should I say, the nods? "Is she supposed to be here?"

"Yes . . . she's scheduled to work."

Okay . . . Again, getting information could be like pulling teeth at times. Without any Novocain and using a pair of rusty pliers. "And it's unusual that she's late?"

"That would be correct." He smiled, like he was proud of me for reaching the proper conclusion.

"Is there any way I can get in touch with her?" I batted my eyelashes, not above using my power to look innocent to get answers. "It's kind of important."

His eyes widened, and he dropped his voice. "It's for Zane, isn't it?"

Did he mean, it's for Zane because he's locked up, or it's for Zane because Zane is one of their endorsers? Either way . . . "Yes, it's for Zane."

"That's what I figured." He scribbled something. "I'd give you her phone number, but she's not answering. Here's her address instead. If you see her, tell her we could really use her help today."

Because it was super busy in here? I didn't even ask.

I took the paper from him and held it in the air. "I'll do that."

Now I had to go find this girl. Because the fact she wasn't at work today only raised more red flags. And what did red flags mean here at the beach?

That danger was on the horizon.

Before I tried to find Bianca, I stopped at my favorite restaurant, The Fatty Shack, to grab a bite to eat. I was starving.

But probably not as hungry as Zane was.

I took my time eating, trying to compose myself and gather my thoughts. With my fish taco salad—minus the tortilla strips—finished, it was time to continue pushing myself forward. Thinking wasn't going to get me very far as this point. I needed to keep asking questions.

Fifteen minutes later, I pulled up to an RV in one of the area's campgrounds. I knew these "resort parks," as many business owners proclaimed them to be, were for more than just vacationers here for a week. Some people made them a permanent home because of the high cost of living in the area. RV living was a cheaper option.

Bianca's RV seemed to fit my expectations of her. There were beads outside the front door. Shimmering purple curtains had been draped at the corners of a small six-by-six deck. Large pieces of driftwood sat on another side of the RV, and broken shells had been placed there, as well as a couple of weathered buoys.

I climbed the steps, moved the strings of beads aside,

and knocked at the door. Two tries later, someone answered.

It wasn't Bianca.

No, it was a redhead with bed-head. I decided that should be a new rap song, but I'd have to ponder some catchy lyrics later, as well as brush up on my beatboxing.

"What do you want?" The woman raked a hand through her hair. I should say, she *attempted* to rake a hand through her hair. Her fingers got stuck halfway through.

"I'm looking for Bianca." I noted the scent of incense floating from inside. In my experience, people used incense for only one thing: to cover up the scent of weed. But I wouldn't jump to conclusions—not yet, at least.

She squinted and pursed her lips. "She's not here."

"When did you see her last?"

"I dunno. Last night around nine." She seemed to wake up a little and stared at me. "Who are you?"

"I'm a friend of a friend. I need to talk to her." *Please buy that. Please buy that. Please buy that.*

If I mentally chanted that enough, maybe it would count for something.

"Yeah, well, like I said, she's not here. Maybe she spent the night with a friend, and she's at work now."

"I went to Slick Ocean first. She never showed up, and she's not answering her phone."

"Hm. That's weird. I don't know where she is." She didn't sound like she cared, either.

"Could I ask you a question?"

"Like what?" An aloof, skeptical look shielded her eyes, as if she realized I might be an enemy.

"I heard she and Morty broke up. Do you know why?"

She relaxed, as if she could handle that question. But she'd been preparing for a much more intense inquiry, hadn't she? I wondered what that might be.

She shrugged. "I just assumed it was so she could date that other guy."

Maybe we were on to something now. "What other guy?"

She released a long, exaggerated breath that filled her cheeks and made a flatulent-like sound as the air escaped through her lips. "Zane Oakley, of course."

Zane? What in the world was going on here?

Chapter Seven

MY THOUGHTS TURNED and turned inside me as I left Bianca's place. My problem was that I usually either talked to Zane or Jackson when I didn't know what to do next. In this case, I couldn't really talk to either because they were pitted against each other.

I needed someone new, and I had just the person.

I pulled up at Beach Combers, the salon owned by Dizzy Jenkins and my former place of employment. In the three months I'd worked there, I hadn't burned anyone's hair off (not by much, at least), tinted any white-haired senior's poof any shade of purple, or totally misunderstood any haircut wishes—like accidentally chopping off ten inches instead of two. I was rather proud of myself, especially since I'd been rusty in my beautician skills and rather accident-prone.

There weren't a lot of cars in the parking lot outside. Unfortunately for Dizzy, I hoped that meant she wasn't busy. Which was awfully selfish of me, but I wanted to talk to her alone.

I walked inside, and the sound of Caribbean-infused Christmas music greeted me. Dizzy loved Christmas music, whatever time of year. And she'd found this new Caribbean mix that she felt justified playing even when we had customers. *It sounds like beach music, doesn't it? It's perfect for this area.*

I hadn't had the heart to argue.

I waved to Winona, one of the new stylists who had been hired for the season. She lived over in Mann's Harbor but commuted here three days a week. Apparently, she raked in decent money by working in the summer and filing for unemployment on the off-season. I wasn't really sure about the ins and outs of it, but apparently a lot of people around here did that.

"Joey Darling, what brings you by? You're not working today, are you?" She smacked her gum like a champ and wore tiny scarves around her neck, which made me think she should audition for a role in *Grease* if haircutting didn't work out.

"Nope. I'm looking for Dizzy."

"She's in the back. Doing some research."

I didn't even ask if I could go see her. I just did.

Dizzy was sitting at the table in the office area, humming to herself while she painted her nails and looked at a magazine.

Dizzy had been married to my uncle for a short time, but he'd passed away two years ago. She was in her fifties and about forty pounds overweight. She dyed her hair a dark brown and piled it high on top of her head. But perhaps it was her blue eyeshadow that got her the most attention. She wore it thick and all the way up to her thinly plucked eyebrows.

I peered over her shoulder and scowled when I saw what she was reading. The *National Instigator*. My nemesis.

"Research?" My voice lilted skeptically with my question.

She put the magazine down and had the decency to blush, at least. "Hairstyles of the rich and famous?"

Her upturned intonation made it clear she was fishing for excuses.

I shrugged, not feeling up to arguing with her. "Sure."

She closed the article she was reading on Starla and blew on her nails instead. "What brings you by? Looking for some extra work?"

"Not today. I need your advice."

Her eyes lit. "Advice? I love giving advice."

"I thought you might." I moved some boxes of hair dye that needed to be inventoried and sat down across from her. "So here's what's happened."

I told her about my day, all the way from finding the body to running into Jackson at Abe's place and trying to track down Bianca. She listened attentively to my every word and made all the proper facial expressions to show she was paying attention.

"What a mess. A horrible, horrible mess." Her eyes lit again. "So what do you need my help with?"

"I have no idea where to go next." I still felt flabbergasted, even as I admitted that out loud. Jackson was questioning Abe, Bianca was MIA, and Zane was looking guiltier with every wave that crashed on the Outer Banks.

"Really?" She folded her hands and nodded slowly,

dramatically thoughtful. "Well, let's see. Abe offered you nothing. Bianca is gone with the wind. Zane claims he's innocent. And Morty is dead—God rest his soul."

"That's correct." It was as if she'd just read my thoughts and reiterated them.

She let out a sigh, looked in the distance, and puckered her lips out, as if in thought.

"I guess I need to find out more information about Morty," I said. "But I don't know how to do that without putting myself in a bad place."

"I know exactly what you can do." Dizzy nodded smugly.

"You do? I mean, what?"

"Well, Morty's best friend is Evan."

"Okay." I had no idea where she was going with this.

"Evan's mom is Annette. Annette organizes one of those rock-hiding groups."

"Rock-hiding groups?" Why in the world would people hide rocks?

"That's right. There are people who paint rocks and hide them all over the town for people to find and enjoy. Anyway, she's having a rock-painting party tomorrow at that new park down the street from Whalebone Junction. You should go."

"That's a great idea."

I knew talking to Dizzy would make everything better. And I'd been right.

Even though I'd told Jackson I'd meet him at his place and then we could ride together to Phoebe's, I had my doubts that he was even going to be able to go. Despite that, I showed up at his house.

He wasn't there.

Of course.

Instead of turning around or heading down to Hatteras myself, I decided to wait for a few minutes. I climbed out of my car so I could enjoy some fresh—though hot—air. Why pay for a sauna when you could step outside?

I crossed my arms and leaned against my red Miata, taking a moment to breathe and gather my thoughts.

As I closed my eyes, a sound—more like a commotion—caught my ear. "Come back here!"

I plucked an eye open and saw a woman dashing through the yard, chasing a dog.

It wasn't just any dog. It was Ripley.

Jackson's dog.

I stared for a minute before coming to my senses and realizing I should help. I bent over and patted my hands against my thighs. "Come here, Ripley."

At once, the Australian shepherd raced toward me. Uh-oh. I braced myself for the impact I knew was coming. It would be like a tidal wave hitting me full force.

Sure enough, Ripley barreled into me, knocking me into the car. As I lost my balance and sank lower, he attacked me with slobbery doggy kisses.

"I'm so sorry!" The woman rushed toward me and stopped, standing in front of me breathlessly. She reached for Ripley's collar, but the dog was determined to make Death by Licking an actual thing.

"Ripley, leave it!" I said.

Jackson had taught me that command.

To my surprise, it worked.

Finally, I managed to stand up. I wiped away the saliva from my cheeks and grimaced.

Ripley couldn't care less. He sat in front of me, wagging his tail and appearing rather pleased with himself. I was pretty sure he'd thought the greeting was welcoming.

I sighed and rubbed his head. "Hey, boy."

"You're Joey Darling," the woman said, a touch of awe to her voice.

I glanced at her for the first time. Earlier she'd been a scramble of limbs and yelling and frantic chasing. But as her features came into focus, I realized this was the new neighbor who was helping Jackson with Ripley on his long workdays.

And she was pretty.

Something Jackson had never mentioned.

Not that he had to. I mean, that would have been awkward to mention to me, right? But still. It felt weird.

She was a honey blonde with porcelain skin and a thin dancer build.

I glanced at her hand. And she wasn't wearing a wedding ring.

How . . . interesting.

"I'm Crista." She extended her hand. "I just moved here from Maryland. I took a teaching job, but it doesn't start until the fall. I figured I could enjoy the beach until then."

"Absolutely. I'm . . . well, you know my name. Joey." I stood and brushed off my knees, elbows, and butt.

She studied me another minute. "So you and Jackson are friends? I had no idea. I mean, I heard rumors you were in the area, but I never guessed this . . ."

I nodded. "We are."

I wanted to say that we were more than friends. But we weren't. Not really. I mean, kind of. It was confusing. Of course, I was a confusable kind of gal.

"Isn't he great?" Crista said. "I've really enjoyed having him as my neighbor."

My throat clenched. Was that . . . jealousy rearing its nasty head inside me? That was ridiculous. I had no reason to feel jealous.

Yet I did.

"I'm sure he's a great neighbor," I finally choked out.

"Oh, he is. He's even shared a hamburger with me a time or two when he was grilling out."

The jealousy flared even brighter and bigger.

This wasn't good. I didn't like jealousy. I didn't like feeling it. I didn't like the insecurity it brought. And I was nearing thirty, so I should be past this.

"Well, I think it's great that you're helping him with Ripley."

"Oh, it's the least I can do. My dad was a cop, so I know all about that schedule."

"Was he?" She and Jackson had something in common. Wasn't that nice?

She nodded. "I know what it's like to live that life. I'll do whatever I can to make things easier for him."

"That's . . . so kind of you." My words were sincere, but I could hear an edge of obligation to them. I'd forced myself to speak them aloud.

But what did Crista mean when she said she'd do

whatever she could to make life easier for him? That wasn't normally the role a neighbor took.

I started to ask her about it, but a shadow crossed me at that moment.

I looked over to see who'd arrived.

Chapter Eight

JACKSON. It was Jackson.

I'd programmed myself to think everything was dangerous when in reality it wasn't. It was the nature of the non-job I was presently doing.

Jackson pulled his truck into the driveway behind my Miata. He climbed out and joined us, looking from me to Crista with a polite nod and then rubbing Ripley's head.

"Have you been a good boy today?" He gave the dog a stern look, seeming to read Ripley's rambunctious eye sparkle.

Ripley barked and sat like an angel.

"Oh, he's been great," Crista said, her voice climbing in pitch and becoming more animated with every word. "I took him down to the sound. Did you know he likes to play fetch there?"

"Yeah, he likes anything that gets him attention." Jackson shifted his gaze from Crista to me again. "I guess the two of you have met?"

I wanted to scowl, but that would make me seem petty. And you know what they say? *Petty is as petty does.*

No, that wasn't right.

Either way, I didn't want to be that person. So instead I nodded.

"We sure did," I said, utilizing my acting skills and sounding pleasant instead of irrational.

"I'm such a huge fan," Crista said, clasping her hands in front of her. "I love *Family Secrets.*"

"Thanks." I was pretty proud of my work in that movie. There'd already been talk of an Oscar nod.

"And I plan on watching *Celebrity Truth or Dare* this week," Crista continued. "I heard you're going to be on."

I remembered my blooper and blushed. "It's really not that exciting. The best part is that all the money won that week went to a charity of our choice. I chose Lone Heart, an organization that supports single parents."

Could I get a lawyer involved and somehow have them not air that episode? Or that part of the episode?

Probably not.

In the meantime, I'd just have to pray that no one would watch. Or that Mel B would get all the attention.

"Well, Ripley is doing great." Crista gave Ripley one more pat and then straightened. "Let me know if you need me to let him out tomorrow."

Jackson smiled warmly. "I'll do that, Crista. Have a great evening."

Something about the way he said the words made another wave of jealousy wash through me.

I had to get a grip.

Once Crista was back on her property, Jackson turned toward me.

"Just let me change, and we can go," Jackson said, almost as if that whole exchange hadn't just happened.

Because he hadn't thought anything of it. Of course. Only neurotic people like me overthought things. The last thing I needed was to go all *Fatal Attraction*. Nope. Nope. And noper.

"You want to wait inside?" Jackson asked.

"I'll stay out here with Ripley." For some reason, I felt like I needed to get on the dog's good side. Ripley needed to like me more than Crista.

Mature, Joey. Really mature.

"Sure thing." Jackson disappeared inside.

As soon as he was gone, I leaned down toward Ripley. "Hey, boy. You still like me, right?"

Ripley licked my face, helping my fears dissolve.

I supposed once you'd been cheated on and told by an ex-spouse that he wished he'd never married you, that other women were prettier and better, and that no one would ever want you once they got to know you, it played with your emotions.

And this was why Jackson and I couldn't date right now. He'd recognized how much baggage I carried, and he knew I needed to move past some of these issues before we'd be ready to date.

But what if he changed his mind? What if Jackson didn't want to wait, especially if he met someone else—someone more perfect? Someone like Crista?

I pushed those thoughts aside. Dwelling on those insecurities wouldn't make anything better right now. In fact, it could spiral into destruction—a place I didn't want to go.

Jackson reappeared a few minutes later wearing some gray shorts and a black T-shirt. He paused in front of me, his eyes glimmering and all those earlier signs of conflict gone.

I supposed it went back to separating his personal and professional life—something he was immensely good at.

Me? Not so much.

It was all personal to me.

He leaned one hand against my car and lingered dangerously close—dangerous for my heart, at least. It thumped out of control at his nearness.

"Are you okay?" he asked.

His voice sounded low and intimate, the kind of tone that made my bones turn to gel.

I considered my response. There was so much I could say. About the case. Crista. Us.

"I'm fine," I said instead.

He stared at me another moment. I saw the green flecks in his eyes. His sexy stubble. The curve of his soft lips.

"Good." He offered me a grin—one I thought was reserved just for me. Then he nodded toward his truck, and the moment broke like a spider web in a hurricane. "Let's get going. Come on, Ripley. You're coming too."

I released the breath I hadn't realized I'd been holding. Jackson did something to my heart that I didn't remember anyone else ever doing. Whatever the reaction, it was thrilling and terrifying at the same time.

Ripley jumped into the backseat, looking ready for whatever adventure awaited.

Somehow, being in the truck with the two of them felt like home. It felt right, like what weekends and time off should be. These moments encompassed what I considered to be the good life. Island life. The perfect life.

Jackson pulled out, and we started down the road. Our windows were down, and a gentle country tune played on the radio. Not only that, but he'd brought out an Izze for me to drink. It was my favorite—a carbonated fruit juice that let me get my soda fix without any soda. He'd been paying attention.

Should I keep things nice and not bring up Zane or the case? Or should I speak what was on my mind?

I started with safe territory. "How are you?"

"It's been busy," Jackson said.

What did that mean? What had he discovered? I so desperately wanted to know.

"So . . ." I twiddled my thumbs a minute. "Did you lock up Abe?"

"The Dare County Sheriff's Department did," Jackson said. "There just happened to be an outstanding warrant for his arrest for failure to appear in court on a disorderly conduct charge."

"Is that right?"

"Plus, he ran from a police officer and resisted arrest, which could also result in a misdemeanor."

"Shame on him." I didn't really care. I wanted to know about this case! "Did he admit to anything concerning Zane?"

"I can't say."

I didn't want to pout, but I might have stuck my lower lip out just a little. "I see."

Jackson glanced at me, his gaze as assessing as always. "You still think Zane is innocent?"

"Until proven guilty. Isn't that what the law says?"

His jaw flexed, like it always did when his thoughts were heavy and serious. "It is. But it's not looking good, Joey."

Chapter Nine

JACKSON STARED STRAIGHT AHEAD at the road, but I could sense his mental wheels were turning. Jackson was not only careful about what he said, but he was also careful about the progression of his thoughts and his assessments of situations. I could learn a few things from him.

"Who do you think we should look at?" he finally asked.

I didn't have to think for very long. "Bianca, of course."

Jackson raised his eyebrows, but his expression otherwise remained unchanged. "Morty's ex-girlfriend?"

I nodded, remembering everything I'd learned about her. My mental review only solidified my suspicion she could be guilty. "The one and only."

"And why do you think we should talk to her?"

That was another easy question. "Because she disappeared. That makes her look guilty."

He remained quiet for a minute before finally saying, "You've been doing your homework."

"Of course I have." I was Joey Darling. I might flub up a lot, but no one could accuse me of not trying.

Jackson stole a glance at me, his green eyes curious. "Anything else you've discovered?"

I shook my head, realizing exactly what was happening here. I crossed my arms to drive home my words. "Oh no. You want me to share what I've learned while doing all my hard work while you're tight lipped? That's not fair."

He looked away, and a smile curled the edge of his lip. "I see."

I decided to try a different approach. "How about this? You show me your clues, I'll show you mine."

He chuckled and ran a hand across his jaw and along the back of his neck. "Tempting, but no."

I frowned. At least I'd tried.

Phoebe lived on the island of Hatteras. In the summer, she ran a dog-sitting and dog-walking business. She lived in a decent-sized house located right on the Pamlico Sound. I'd been here a couple of times before to paddle-board on the calm waters.

As soon as Jackson and I got there, he took Ripley to the water to stretch and play fetch.

I, on the other hand, knocked and then let myself into the mudroom. Phoebe greeted me at the top of the steps that led to the living area upstairs.

"Joey, you made it!" Phoebe gave me a quick hug.

It might sound awkward, but Phoebe was Jackson's deceased wife's sister. It surprisingly wasn't weird at all, and that was mostly attributed to the fact that Phoebe was down to earth.

Phoebe was the epitome of beach life. She was a petite blonde who didn't need makeup or any hair products—usually she just braided her hair and it looked perfect. She was slim, loved the beach, and had a laid-back attitude that made her easy to get along with but sometimes hard to read.

"I'm so glad you could come, Joey." She ushered me toward the kitchen. "It's been too long."

I still saw her at Oh Buoy, the smoothie shop I liked to frequent and one of her places of employment. But I hadn't been going there as often now that I wasn't working at Beach Combers as much. This was also prime dog-sitting season for Phoebe.

"I'm going to grab everything, and we can head down to the beach." She pulled out a cooler. "The rest of the gang is going to meet us down there. It's the perfect time. The sun is just starting to set."

"I've been wanting to do a beach bonfire. Glad we finally can."

She'd told me earlier that she'd invited a few of her other friends, including Robbie, a guy I felt pretty certain liked her. I looked forward to seeing them interact. But until then, I turned toward the kitchen window and stole a glance at the Pamlico Sound.

The water looked choppy today with little whitecaps dotting the normally peaceful expanse. I wondered if the storm brewing out to sea had stirred them up.

Phoebe opened the fridge but paused and squinted at me. "What happened to your back?"

My eyes widened as I turned away from the window. "My back?"

She abandoned the fridge, turned me around, and narrowed her eyes. "You have these weird polka dots there."

"What are you talking about? My shirt is solid black." I tried to glance over my shoulder, but I didn't have a great view of my backside. Phoebe was making me nervous.

"Not on your shirt. On your skin." She leaned closer to examine the spots.

"I have polka dots on my skin? Like chicken pox?" Alarm raced through me.

She twisted her neck, as if confused. "No, these are light brown and dime shaped."

"Dime shaped?" All of a sudden, it hit me. My stomach dropped at the realization. "Oh no."

"Oh no what?" Phoebe popped her gaze back up to meet mine.

I squeezed the skin between my eyes as I reviewed the events leading up to this. "I wore this shirt with little holes in it today."

"Little holes?"

"It's a long story, but I was assured the top was very stylish." I frowned, remembering my conversation with Miranda Worthington about it. *It's totally a new trend. You'll be fashion forward, and the magazines will love it. You'll do for this shirt what that crazy aunt of yours did for blue eyeshadow.*

"Okay . . ." Phoebe said.

"But I was outside a lot today. I didn't even think about putting sunscreen on."

"So you got a tan wherever there was a hole." A smile played on her lips. "Well, you're making a statement. There's nothing wrong with that."

I closed my eyes. And tonight of all nights, I'd worn

a nearly backless shirt. It was another fashion piece that was stylish, something that Miranda had recommended. Little black straps ran across the middle and it gently draped, which would have looked elegant any other time. But not when I'd just given myself the weirdest suntan ever.

I was a walking disaster.

Phoebe continued gathering hot dogs and supplies for s'mores. As she did, she casually said, "I heard about Zane."

My thoughts turned from picturing myself on the latest issue of the *National Instigator* to my friend. I frowned as I remembered everything that had happened. "Everyone has apparently."

"I can't believe it." She added an ice pack to the cooler.

"Neither can I."

She offered a side glance as she rearranged a few items so everything could fit. "I don't like Zane—you know our history—but I don't think he would do this."

"Me neither."

Her motions slowed along with her words. "Unless he was high at the time."

That stopped my thoughts cold. "What do you mean?"

She paused. "You've never seen him high."

"No . . ." Thank goodness.

"He's a different person, Joey. He's mean."

I swallowed hard, not liking that thought. I preferred the happy-go-lucky Zane. "So you think he could have done this?"

Phoebe shrugged. "I'm just saying."

I didn't like where this was going, but it was good for

me to know. I needed the facts, needed to keep them in mind.

But what if I was going out on a limb here and it turned out Zane was guilty? What if I ended up discovering evidence that helped put him behind bars? Justice and loyalty collided inside me.

This was all so complicated.

I crossed my arms and leaned against the counter, hoping we still had a few minutes before Jackson came back inside.

"Did you know Morty?" I asked.

"Everyone around here knows Morty." She closed the lid of the cooler. "And in case you were going to ask, he's trouble. Drugs do horrible things to people, and unfortunately for some groups of people, drugs are just a part of the beach lifestyle. You surf. You feel good. You get high or drunk to celebrate. I don't get it, but it's what I've seen repeated over and over again."

"I see." I followed behind her as she lowered the cooler—which had wheels—and began pulling it behind her toward the steps.

"And people always think they can break the chains of addiction in their lives. And they can. It's entirely possible. But it's hard. So hard. It takes a lifelong dedication to stick with it. One slipup, and you're back to where you started."

"You think that's what happened to Zane?"

She paused before going down the stairs, her full attention on me and a somber look on her face. "I have no idea. I don't keep up with him. I don't want to know. No offense."

"I'm not offended."

"Back to your question about Morty. He and Billy

Corbina were cut from the same cloth. You want to look into Morty's life? Look at Billy."

That wasn't a good sign. "You think I'm looking into this?"

"Aren't you?"

I shrugged, realizing she easily had me pegged. "Maybe. Well, yes. I am."

"And what does Jackson think about this?" She shifted her weight from one leg to the other but remained in place.

I thought about our terse conversation earlier and frowned. "He's not a fan."

"Because it's personal. You're not going to be objective."

"Nor is he," I pointed out.

"But he will have an easier time putting his emotions aside. You know it's true." She gave me the one-raised-eyebrow look.

I couldn't even argue. Jackson was definitely better at the whole self-control thing. I couldn't even stick with my diet plan for one day. For example, I'd probably eat a hot dog tonight—even though every day I vowed to eat only raw food.

What if the hot dog was raw? Hmm . . . food for thought.

"Anyway, I'm sure Jackson doesn't want you involved," Phoebe said. "Not if Billy is a part of this. Billy is nothing but trouble. If I were you, I'd stay far away also."

I'd heard that before.

But staying far away from things was so hard for me.

Chapter Ten

So far, the evening had been a blast. We'd played some low-pressure volleyball. I'd chased Ripley in and out of the waves. Then we sat down for hot dogs and conversation.

Yes, I'd eaten a hot dog. Actually, two hot dogs. I'd also made a s'more, licking every last ounce of gooey goodness from my melted marshmallows off my fingers —but only because I didn't have anything to wash my hands with.

We'd ended by sitting around the campfire and chatting and telling stories. There were eight of us all together. Most of the crowd was new, though I'd seen some before.

Robbie was there. I hadn't been around much until this evening, but I decided I liked him. He was kind of shy, but he was always stealing glances at Phoebe. She either didn't notice or didn't care. I couldn't figure them out.

But I wanted to.

"So you're an actress, right?" a guy named Art

asked. He apparently owned a hamburger shop down south in Frisco.

"Last time I checked," I said with a smile.

"I've always wanted to ask an actress this question," he continued.

"What's that?"

"What are onscreen kisses like?"

I chuckled, halfway relieved that the question was actually answerable. I just never knew what some people were going to ask. "Oh, they're terribly awkward most of the time."

"Tell us more," Phoebe said. "The average person— like all of us—has no idea."

I thought back to the many onscreen kisses I'd done. Twelve, to be exact. And yes, I'd counted them. Mostly because I got anxiety attacks before each one.

"Well, on the big screen, they look super romantic, right?" I said. "But filming them is a beast. The more romantic the kiss, the more technical it is. You have all these people watching, and lights are on you, and the director is telling you how to kiss. *Move your head this way. Turn so that your body's facing the camera more.* It's horrible. And then there's the bad breath."

"The bad breath?" someone else asked.

"That's the beauty of the big screen. You never smell anything. It makes people seem superhuman. I did this one kiss in *Yesterday's Tomorrow*—it was my first onscreen kiss—and it was horrible. Josh Harris, my costar, had just eaten cheese, and I absolutely wanted to gag."

"Well, that takes some of the mystery out of it," Phoebe said.

Everyone laughed.

"Believe me—onscreen kisses are far from romantic."

Jackson said nothing beside me, and I wondered what he was thinking. This wasn't the time to ask.

Art spoke instead. "So, it's pretty crazy about Morty, isn't it?"

"I heard he quit his job at Willie's," someone else said.

"I saw Billy trolling around on a new boat," Art said. "Maybe they came into some moolah together."

"His dad probably bought it for him," Phoebe added with a knowing shrug of her eyebrows.

I glanced at Jackson, and I could see him listening to everything. Yet he said nothing. Offered nothing. Gave no indication he knew a thing.

"I heard his dad cut him off," Robbie said.

Interesting. Robbie didn't seem like the type who would know something like that. Did he and Billy have some kind of history together? I didn't know.

But I added one more theory to my list.

Possible windfall.

As darkness settled around us, people began to fade—including Phoebe, who'd taken Ripley back with her.

But Jackson and I remained. I wasn't complaining. I wanted some time to chat one on one with him.

Before we chatted, we listened to the waves crash. We let the salty air wrap us like a heavy blanket. We enjoyed the feel of the soft sand beneath our feet.

I watched the fire, mesmerized by the flames. By the

crackles. By the warmth it provided as the evening had grown chilly.

I shivered, and Jackson grabbed a blanket and draped it around my shoulders. Then he scooted closer and slipped his arm around my waist.

Warmth oozed through every bone in my body at his touch and his nearness and his masculinity . . . well, at nearly everything about him.

"No talk about work, deal?" He stared at the fire, seeming as mesmerized by it as I felt.

That would be disappointing if I'd thought he would actually open up about this investigation. But I knew he wouldn't, so there was no need to argue. "Deal."

We said nothing for a while longer. And saying nothing felt perfect.

I used to say that was the ultimate test of a relationship—when you could enjoy simply being together. When there was no urge to fill the silence with meaningless words. When the quiet didn't feel awkward.

"I feel like I can breathe when I'm out here." I closed my eyes as the breeze kissed my face.

"Breathing is good."

I elbowed him. "I know that. You know what I mean."

Jackson paused, but only for a second. "So I guess onscreen kisses are just a part of your job, huh?"

Surprise rippled through me. He had been listening . . . and possibly even been troubled by that earlier conversation. "I guess you could say that. Does that bother you?"

He shrugged. "I . . . I don't know. I didn't think about it much until tonight."

"I promise there's nothing romantic about them."

"Yeah, you said that."

I heard a touch of doubt in his voice. "You don't believe me?"

"I didn't say that." He released a breath. "But it is a weird thought."

"I think it would be strange if I saw you kissing someone while you were undercover."

He let out a half chuckle. "I wouldn't do that while I was undercover."

I didn't know what to say that hadn't already been stated.

"I have no acting gigs lined up right now, so I guess it's a nonissue." I snapped my fingers. "Oh wait—we're talking about work. You broke your own rule!"

He chuckled, but the sound faded like the dying flames in front of us. "Fair enough. Okay, I have a different question. What are you thinking for the future, Joey? What are your goals? Your plans? Not career wise, per se. Life wise."

"Thank you for asking me about me and not Hollywood."

"Really, of all the things I like about you, Hollywood is nowhere near the top. I like you because of you. You make me laugh. You make me want to pull my hair out . . . you make me look forward to each new day."

I looked up at him—at his face as it glowed orange near the embers of the fire. Before I realized what I was doing, I traced my thumb across his jaw. "Those are the sweetest words ever."

"Well, what can I say? I'm a sweet kind of guy."

I laughed. Though Jackson was sweet, that word seemed foreign to attach to him. No, he seemed like all muscles and toughness on the outside, but he had a gentleness beneath all that.

His eyes warmed as he stared at me. My breath caught as I waited, anticipated, longed to feel his mouth against mine. I could see it in his gaze—he wanted it too.

But his lips hit my forehead instead of my mouth.

I sighed.

I was disappointed yet not disappointed. I could appreciate someone with conviction and integrity. I'd appreciate it even more once my heart stopped pounding out of control.

I leaned onto his shoulder and watched the flames flicker, the gentle breeze stirring the blaze. A family down the shore searched with their flashlights for ghost crabs, the kids squealing with delight and running after something with their nets. The stars shined bright over-head, illuminating the darkness.

This place felt like heaven on earth.

"How are things going with Eric?" Jackson asked.

My peaceful feelings faded at the mention of my ex. But this was a good conversation to have. Eric was a major reason Jackson and I were taking things slowly.

"Honestly, things are going better," I said. "I can't complain. It helps that I don't have to see him or talk to him anymore."

"You did manage to skip your anniversary. I'm pretty impressed by that."

"Best decision ever. It was very healing, in a strange way. I know I can't erase that time in my life, but I can definitely learn from it. It's going to make me stronger—a better person in the end."

"I'm proud of you, Joey."

I tried not to glow too much under his compliment. The nice thing about compliments from Jackson was that they were sincere. Most of the time, people were nice to me because they wanted something.

"I find it hard to believe, but Eric's career very much may be going to pot right now," I continued. "I didn't think it could get worse—I thought his actions would give him notoriety. But from what I've heard, no one wants to touch him with a ten-foot pole. We'll see if that changes."

"Maybe that will be a wake-up call to him," Jackson said.

"Maybe."

Suddenly, that feeling returned. The feeling of being watched.

As my muscles tensed, I looked around. The light from the campfire made it hard to see anything else beyond its glow.

"What is it?" Jackson asked.

Just then, my gaze found the source of my alarm. The outdoor light from a nearby house illuminated a face.

It was the man. My stalker. Leonard Shepherd.

And he was hiding in the sea oats behind us.

Chapter Eleven

LEONARD MUST HAVE HAD a car tucked away close to the walking path. Because nearly as soon as Jackson disappeared over the sand dune, he returned. He was shaking his head and looking altogether displeased with himself.

I pulled the blanket closer, chilled to the bone at the daunting possibilities facing me. I hadn't even begun to scratch the surface as to what those might be. "Well?"

Jackson lowered himself beside me. "He got away. By the time I crested the dune, he was already at the end of the street. He was in some kind of truck. It was too dark to make out the details, and the license plate was either gone or covered up. I already called it in, just in case any officers on duty come across it."

I frowned, already knowing that probably wouldn't happen. Leonard had been eluding the police for a while now. "Although it's not a crime to sit on a sand dune. That's what he'll argue if he's caught."

"It's not. But the fact that he ran makes it seem suspicious."

"I agree."

My soul still felt unsettled. Leonard Shepherd was trouble, and he seemed to be focused on me.

Jackson turned toward me. "You have any idea who that guy was?"

Oh, had I not mentioned that to him? "Maybe."

"What's that mean?" Jackson asked.

"Well, I saw someone earlier today—when I left the police station. He reminded me of . . . well, he reminded me of the man I had a restraining order on in California. Leonard Shepherd."

He blinked with what appeared to be surprise. "You're just now telling me that you may have seen Leonard Shepherd today?"

I shrugged. "You seemed really busy. Besides, the thought is crazy."

"For most people, I might agree. For you? It's not so crazy." He let out a small sigh. "I'm going to look into it first thing in the morning when I get back to my office."

"Okay." I had a feeling this wouldn't end easily, with a simple arrest. I could feel it in my bones that Leonard was planning something. The man was calculating, which made him even scarier.

I knew a limited amount of facts about him based on my earlier restraining order against him. He was thirty-three and never married. From what I'd heard, he was unable to hold a steady job—and his jobs were usually the minimum-wage type. Mostly fast-food joints.

Despite that, I'd heard that he was amazingly smart. He'd graduated high school at the top of his class and had been offered a place at MIT. But he'd been a socially awkward misfit with a slew of other problems.

"How does this always happen to you, Joey?"

Jackson hooked his arm around my neck and pulled me to him.

I didn't resist. I fell into his warm embrace and rested my head against his chest, tucked under his chin. This was my happy place.

"I have a knack for these things," I murmured.

"I'd say you do." He paused.

I listened to his heartbeat. It was comforting and steady and reliable enough to ease my tense muscles. If only every moment of my life felt this easy.

In the silence, Zane popped into my mind. Despite all the questions I had for my friend, I began thinking about him sitting in a jail cell, and my heart panged with compassion.

This had started with him. He'd asked for my help. And now I was wading through murky waters for him. Would I end up sinking or swimming?

After a few minutes, Jackson cleared his throat. "I really wish you'd stay away from this investigation, Joey."

It was like he'd read my mind and knew exactly what I'd been thinking about. "You say that every time." Unfortunately, this was a recurring theme in our relationship.

"This time I mean it."

"You didn't the other times?"

"I didn't say that. But this time . . . I don't want you to get in over your head."

"You must know something about this that I don't. Something serious."

He remained silent.

I figured he would but hoped he wouldn't.

"Let's get you home, Joey."

He took my hand, and we walked across the dune.

At least the day had ended well. Sometimes that was all you could ask for.

It had been so sweet of Jackson to drop me off at my place last night. But this morning, as I grabbed my car keys and stepped outside into the parking lot, I found my space was empty.

My Miata was still at Jackson's place.

Had that been his grand plan this whole time? If I didn't have a vehicle, it would be much harder to investigate. And if I didn't investigate, then I would stay out of trouble—and out of his hair.

That plan was not out of the realm of possibility.

But this was a problem because I had a rock-painting thingamajig to attend.

I stared at my empty parking space and sighed. Should I call Jackson? Uber? Maybe I could just walk, but I'd totally have to change out of these strappy sandals if I did that.

"Problem?" someone said behind me.

I turned around and saw Winston Corbina standing at the base of the stairs.

Winston Corbina owned this entire complex and lived above me. For that matter, he owned a lot of properties and buildings in this area and had his own little real estate empire. And just as a fun fact, he looked like Burt Reynolds's younger brother.

He also had a connection to my father, who was missing. I suspected he knew more than he was letting on.

And right now he was looking at me, waiting for a response to his one-word question about my problems. Where did I even start? My career, my poor fashion choices, my diet?

I knew none of those things were what he was talking about. Instead, I nodded toward the empty parking space.

"I just realized I left my car somewhere," I told him. "It was late when I got in, and I wasn't thinking everything through."

Story of my life.

He tossed me something, and I miraculously caught it in the air. I glanced at my hand, unsure *what* exactly I'd just caught, and I saw . . . keys.

"Take one of my cars," he said. "I have plenty. More than plenty."

I stared at Winston, wondering if he was serious.

He seemed to read my thoughts and said, "Yes, I'm serious."

The man obviously had no idea about my accident history. "I couldn't possibly."

"Sure you can." He nodded toward a yellow car in the distance and winked. "Have yourself some fun."

Without waiting for my response or giving me the chance to hand him his keys back, he climbed into another car—a red Mercedes SUV—and pulled away. That left me staring at those keys. And that yellow car. A Corvette.

Should I?

I didn't really have much choice if I wanted to go anywhere today. On one hand, I didn't want Winston Corbina doing me any favors. He might think I owed him something. On the other hand, I wanted to investigate, and this was the easiest solution.

With a shrug, I climbed into Winston's sports car. I paused once inside and let the soothing smell of leather surround me. This car was nice. Extravagantly nice.

And probably way out of my league when it came to what I could handle. But I'd been handed an opportunity, and I shouldn't back down.

I cranked the engine, and the vehicle roared to life. I halfway expected it to morph into a Transformer or something else equally dramatic, but it didn't. Of course. Because those things only happened in Hollywood.

I drove it around the parking lot a few times to get a feel for how to handle the ride, and then when I felt 25 percent more confident, finally started toward the rock-painting event.

The location was just down the road from my condo, at a little park with a fancy playground and plenty of green space. I'd driven past before but never stopped.

After I found parking—as far away from any other vehicles as I could be—I climbed out, walked toward the crowds and festivities, and soaked everything in with a touch of awe.

This was more than just some people out with their rocks.

There were entire families here, and rows and rows of tables set up on the grass. People gathered there and laughed with paintbrushes in hand. Other kids walked around with snow cones. A man with a guitar played across the lawn.

I hoped I could find some answers here. Because otherwise, I had no idea where to look.

Chapter Twelve

"JOEY DARLING! I'm so glad you're here!" someone said behind me.

I turned and saw Mayor Allen standing there with a grin on his face. He was a short man with a rotund build and a bald head. He also talked with a little lisp, and despite the fact that his every move was motivated by how things could add to his political gain, I still liked him.

He loved me. Like *loved* me loved me. Mostly because I'd brought attention to his little city, which seemed to be the sole purpose of his existence. I didn't want to know. I didn't even ask.

As long as he let me tag along on police investigations, I was okay with his exuberance for all things Joey.

"Who doesn't love painting rocks?" I finally said.

I still had no idea what his was about. I should have done some research, but I'd been so busy yesterday. Then I'd gotten home and fallen in bed, totally exhausted.

And now here I was.

"Exactly!" He nodded toward someone with a camera in the distance. "You mind if we get a few pictures of you here?"

"Not at all."

He leaned closer and dramatically offered a side glance and half-eyebrow raise. "Have you thought about tweeting the event?"

"It's totally on my to-do list." I just put it on there.

"Great minds think alike."

"That's why the two of us are on the same page so often, right?" I grinned, trying to cover my total cluelessness about this. I must have done a good job, because the mayor grinned back at me, his face absolutely beaming.

"You know I think of you as our little local treasure," he said.

"You're too kind." No, really. He was. I wasn't exactly local, but I had been in town for several months, so whatever worked for him. "I guess I should get busy, huh?"

"Yes. I can't wait to see your painting skills."

"Painting skills?" I didn't actually have to paint, did I? I mean, I could just slather a few colors on the rocks and call it a day. Better yet, I would call it abstract art.

"Have fun!"

I stepped toward one of the tables in the distance. Before I reached it, my eyes connected with someone walking in the same direction.

Crista.

For some reason, my stomach clenched at the sight of her. She spotted me just about the same time, and a big smile lit her face. She reached me and paused, as if ready to chat for a while.

Who would have thought I'd run into so many people I knew here?

"Joey!" She grinned, showing her perfect teeth and a warm smile. "I had no idea you were into rock painting."

"Oh, I'm totally into it." What was rock painting again?

"How fun. Someone would flip out if they discovered a rock painted by you. Wait till word of this gets out."

"You think?" They might change their minds when they saw my painting skills.

"Oh, I totally think. Actually, I know."

"I'm sure the mayor will use that to his advantage in whatever way he can."

"I'm sure he will." She smiled but it faded. "Did you and Jackson have fun last night? His truck pulled up awfully late."

Nosy much?

Since I didn't think quickly on my feet, I found myself answering her. "Yeah, he dropped me off at home, but I forgot my car was at his place. I'll need to go get that later on today." I had no idea why I felt the need to explain that, but I did.

"I think it's really cool that the two of you are friends."

We began walking beside each other. I wanted to take off in a sprint like *The Running Man* fighting for his life. In other words, I wanted to avoid this conversation because I could sense turbulence on the horizon.

"He's a great guy," I finally said.

"Yeah, I've noticed." She slowed her steps and turned awkwardly toward me. The breeze kicked up and brought with it the scent of strawberry cream and rainbows. "Can I ask a strange question?"

"Sure." But I mentally braced myself for it. If someone asked you if they could ask you something before asking you whatever it was they wanted to ask, it was never a good sign.

"Are the two of you dating?"

How did I even begin to answer that? Jackson and I were so complicated. I couldn't exactly say, "No, we're not dating, but we kind of are. We just need some time first." That explanation was too convoluted.

"No, we're not," I finally said. But the words felt like a lie as they left my lips.

Her shoulders seemed to slump with relief, and she grinned. "I see. That's good to know. Because I don't meet guys like Jackson very often, but I didn't want to overstep."

I opened my mouth to explain but paused, unsure what exactly I should say. I didn't want to sound like one of those territorial females. But still, I had to say *something*.

"Well," I started.

Before I could finish, two other women came up and began chatting with Crista about painted rocks. From what I gathered they'd be teachers together here in the fall.

The next thing I knew, they were gone. And I hadn't clarified.

Wasn't that just great? Had I just given Crista my blessing to date Jackson?

Welcome to my life.

Dizzy had told me that Morty's best friend Evan's mom would be here.

I had to keep those connections straight in my head. The bad news was twofold: not only had I failed to look into what painted rocks really were, but I hadn't looked up what this woman looked like either. Nor did I know her last name. So I was going to have to find her some other way.

For once, luck was on my side.

I spotted a man around Morty's age whom I'd seen before at Willie Wahoo's. He chatted with a woman old enough to be his mom, and their body language gave off a mother/son vibe—she looked bossy, and he looked like he needed something.

Finally, the woman slipped some cash into his hand, and the familiar guy smiled, kissed her cheek, and walked away.

They definitely appeared to be mother and son.

As soon as he was gone, I walked over to that table and began looking at the rocks and paints laid out there.

"So glad to have you here today," the woman said, sorting through some paintbrushes and organizing them by the size of their tips.

"I'm glad to be here," I said. "What a great turnout. This event totally . . . rocks."

I smiled with amusement at myself.

"Well, yes it does." She finally glanced up and did a double take. "Oh my goodness. You're Joey Darling!"

"I am."

"The mayor just swung by and said you were here." Her full attention was suddenly on me. "I'm Annette, and I'm in charge of the shindig."

"Nice to meet you, Annette."

"It's a good thing I think quickly on my feet, because I have an idea."

"An idea?" I didn't like the start of this. Joey Darling, rock painting, and ideas didn't fit well together.

And what about finding answers? Was I going to get sidetracked . . . again?

Chapter Thirteen

"THAT'S RIGHT. What do you think about this? You can paint some rocks,"—Annette pointed at me with a handful of paintbrushes—"and we'll post them online with a *JoeyRocks* hashtag. Whoever finds your rocks will feel like they've found a special prize—think of it like the golden egg at an Easter egg hunt. People will go crazy over it."

That didn't sound that bad. I mean, Easter egg hunts were fun. "Sure. I can do that."

"Oh, that would be wonderful. We try to paint kind messages to encourage the people who find them," she continued. "I mean, different people paint rocks for different reasons. But that's my favorite. You just never know when someone will find a rock with a message on it just when they need a reminder of those very words."

"That actually sounds really cool." It really did.

"We're charging five dollars per rock here today, and any proceeds we get from this event go to the We Can Fight Cancer Fund. It's a horrible disease. I lost my mom to it three years ago." Her face tightened with grief, and water flashed in her eyes before she blinked the moisture away.

"I'm so sorry," I said. "Cancer is a horrible disease that's claimed way too many lives."

"We're hoping to raise twenty thousand to donate to local victims who need financial assistance," she continued. "Families don't need financial strains on top of everything else they're going through."

"Absolutely."

"I know it seems like a simple little activity—rock painting—but I'm hoping this simple little activity will make a big impact on families who are in need."

"I think that's wonderful. You know—whatever amount you raise, I'll match it." Had I just said that? I really needed to check my bank account before I made promises like that.

But this was a good cause. And I did have more paychecks coming in finally.

I could totally swing it.

Her face brightened. "Oh, would you? That would be wonderful. And a great incentive for people. So this event goes on all weekend and then again next week. Right before it ends, we'll announce how much we raised. Could you be here for the announcement?"

"Of course." I mentally reviewed my schedule. I could . . . right?

She handed me some rocks and waved someone over. "Paint to your heart's content. We'll get some pictures because people always respond better with pictures."

"How'd you get started in this?" I picked up a paintbrush and desperately wished I had some ideas of what to paint. I glanced over at other people who were painting and saw some of their images.

Horses. Lighthouses. Sea turtles.

Some were fancy. Some were simple. Some people were skilled with a brush. Others were just having fun.

I nibbled my lip, trying to think quickly.

"I found a rock that said, 'There's always hope.' I was feeling pretty hopeless at the time, and those words just lifted my load. I know it sounds crazy, but it's true."

"It doesn't sound crazy at all."

I grabbed a bottle of blue and squirted it on a plate, copying some people down the row. "Was that your son you were talking to when I walked up?"

Sound casual, Joey. Casual.

"It was. Evan." She shook her head. "He's a piece of work. If he wasn't my son . . ."

"Sounds like you've had some challenges." I painted a line on the rock, which was already coated with a layer of white. I had no idea what I'd do with the line, but it was a starting point.

"We have. He got into the wrong crowd. Not only that, but his best friend died yesterday."

I gasped. "Is he the man everyone's been talking about? Morty Somebody?"

She nodded, her lips pressed in a frown. "That's right. He and Morty . . . they were two peas in a pod. A dangerous pod."

"What do you think happened to Morty? I thought this area was so safe."

"It is safe. Usually. And I have no idea. All I know is that I woke up in the middle of the night two days ago.

Evan and Morty were in the house. I heard their voices. And they were talking to someone with an Australian accent . . . I think. Their conversation sounded heated."

My pulse spiked. "You'd never heard this guy before?"

"No, never. I thought I knew most of his friends. And it wasn't a guy. It was a girl."

"What do you think it was about?"

"I have no idea. But the two of them have been acting secretive lately. They've had more money than usual too. Whenever I tried to bring it up, they got all quiet and told me that I'm imagining things and that the summer season is when they make most of their money. Et cetera, et cetera, et cetera." She rolled her eyes. "I just stopped asking."

It certainly sounded like drugs to me.

I didn't want to ask the next question, but I was going to anyway. "Does Evan hang out with Zane Oakley, by chance?"

"Zane? Yes, he's been over a few times. They all grew up around here. They all got into trouble together. I thought their paths were changing, but I guess old habits are hard to break." She waved her hand in the air. "Anyway, I'm sure you don't want to hear about all this. What are you painting?"

Oh, I so did want to hear about all this. But instead, I looked down at my rock. I'd painted a little beach scene, and it didn't look half-bad.

"Now maybe you can just add some words," she suggested. "I think the paint should be dry enough, thanks to the heat out here."

"Of course." But what words should I add?

I remembered something Jackson had said to me not too long ago. *Life doesn't have to be perfect to be great.*

That phrase had stuck with me. I grabbed a Sharpie and scribbled in my neatest writing those words on the beach scene there. When I looked at it again, I was rather pleased with the end result.

"Oh, that's just beautiful," Annette said. "People are going to love that. Make more, please."

I decided to write more phrases and pieces of wisdom on my other rocks. Wisdom from my dad.

Bee your best. (I painted a bee.)

Keep the faith. (I painted a mountain.)

Love always. (I painted a heart.)

Hope floats. Rocks don't. (I painted water.)

Okay, my dad didn't say that last one. But I wrote it anyway because it made me laugh. Maybe it would make someone else laugh too.

I smiled for the camera, signed some autographs, and made a big deal out of some of my favorite rock painters' creations.

Then I got Annette's contact information so we could be in touch about where I'd hide these. With that, I left. At least I'd learned something—about rocks and about Morty.

As I was headed down the road, lights flashed in my rearview mirror.

It was a cop.

Really? I was being pulled over?

I let out a sigh and stopped on the side of the road.

Just as I rolled down my window, I spotted an officer standing there, and gawked.

"Jackson?"

"Joey?" He tugged down his sunglasses, as if his eyes were deceiving him. "Why are you driving this car?"

"Because I left mine at your place. Remember?"

"This is Winston Corbina's car," he said, as if I didn't know.

"Yeah, he let me borrow it. So why did you pull me over? And since when do you pull people over?"

His gaze darkened, and I knew there was more to this story. "I pulled you over because you kept crossing the center line. And I can pull people over when I need to."

"I've never known you to pull anyone over. Like ever." He wasn't a highway patrol officer.

"It's my prerogative."

There was more to this. I was sure. I'd always suspected that Jackson knew more about my father's disappearance than he could let on and that he suspected Winston was somehow involved. But out of respect for his job, I kept my mouth shut.

I figured he'd tell me when he could. And I also figured that maybe I didn't want to know. What if Jackson knew something devastating? Maybe it was better to keep hope alive. And floating. Unlike rocks.

"I totally wasn't crossing the center line," I said.

"You totally were. Why do you think all those people were honking at you?"

"Because they recognize me from my movies?" As my words left my lips, I realized how feeble they sounded.

Jackson gave me a look that said it all. He thought I was crazy.

"By the way, did you really reenact a scene from *Chariots of Fire* while you were at the crime scene yesterday?" Jackson asked.

My cheeks heated. "Why would you think that?"

"It popped up on my online newsfeed this morning."

I should have known one of those reporters might have been close by. "I got a little bored."

"I'd say."

"It could have been worse. I could have grabbed you and done the scene in *From Here to Eternity*."

Something lit in his eyes, and I had the impression he liked that idea.

"You're a piece of work, Joey." He shook his head. "Listen, since I caught up with you, I thought you might want to know that I followed up on Leonard Shepherd again to see if anything changed since I last looked into him."

I swallowed hard, suddenly uncomfortable. "Okay. And?"

"As you probably remember, he was locked up for assault and battery about a year ago, but he got out on a parole."

I held my breath, waiting for him to continue.

"I called his parole officer, and he's gone. But we both knew that, right?"

I nodded, but my head felt a little woozy. "He disappeared around five months ago. Right about the time I moved to the Outer Banks."

"Right. He doesn't have any credit cards, so whatever he's doing right now, he's using cash. He also doesn't have a car, so we have no plates to trace. But I've put someone on it. If he's still in this area, we're going to find him."

"Thanks, Jackson."

I considered what I'd just learned during my rock-painting venture. Part of me didn't want to share it—it wasn't like Jackson was sharing anything with me—but I knew I had to.

"There was a woman meeting with Morty and his best friend, Evan, two nights ago," I blurted. "She had a possible Australian accent."

Jackson's eyes widened, as if he recognized something about what I said. "Who told you that?"

"Evan's mom."

"When did you talk to her?" He stopped and shook his head. "Never mind."

"You know something." I gave him a challenging stare.

He gave it right back to me. "I told you before, Joey, that you need to leave this alone. And until we locate this Leonard Shepherd guy, you need to watch your back."

"And I have to hide some rocks, so it sounds like I have a lot going on today."

"What?" Confusion laced his eyes.

"Never mind."

He sighed. "Listen, how about if I drive you back to your car?"

"But I have a Corvette." I rubbed the dashboard. "I'm not even a car enthusiast, but . . . it's a Corvette."

"Joey . . ."

He didn't like Winston Corbina. He hadn't been in favor of me moving into his condo complex either.

"What I really want to do is some more NHPD Blue tweets. I feel like I'm slacking on the job."

He rubbed his jaw. "Somehow, I have a feeling if you're not with me, then you're just going to get in trouble."

I shrugged but said nothing.

"Give the car back, and we'll talk."

Chapter Fourteen

JACKSON WAS GOING to let me help with the investigation. I couldn't believe it, nor could I wait to get started.

I dropped off Winston Corbina's car, as promised. Winston wasn't home, so I'd have to wait until later to return his keys. Then Jackson took me to his house to pick up my car and asked me to come down to the station in an hour.

That gave me just enough time to visit Zane.

I needed to talk to my friend, to figure out how he was doing and to see if he was willing to tell me anything new. Because I felt sure he had more to tell me —if only he would. I had lots and lots of questions also.

Miraculously, I arrived at the jail during visiting hours. Since I'd never really visited a jail before, I hadn't even thought about the rules—other than knowing I couldn't bring a cake with a file baked into it.

After going through the process, I finally got to talk to Zane. A piece of Plexiglas was between us, and I had to use a phone, but at least we could have a conversation.

I stared at him a minute. My friend looked awful.

Any tan he'd sported was now gone, and a pallor replaced it. His eyes didn't have a sparkle. Even his hair had lost its bounce.

Immediately, I missed our times of talking about Bob Ross and drinking smoothies. He was my carefree friend with an adventurous spirit.

But all of that had been taken away faster than a riptide pulling someone to sea.

His bloodshot eyes met mine. "I didn't expect to see you."

I gripped the phone harder. "You're my friend. Of course I'm going to come see you. How are you?"

He sat there stoically but didn't say anything. I waited and then realized I needed to continue, with or without him.

"I heard the gun is yours," I started.

"I bought it for protection." His voice sounded listless and lacked its normal animation.

"I heard your hands tested positive for gunshot residue." These were subjects I didn't want to bring up, but I had to. I couldn't pretend these facts didn't exist when they so clearly did.

"I was at the range earlier that day. Jackson should be able to verify that pretty easily."

I made a mental note of that information. "What about the brick of cocaine found in your room?"

"I have no idea. Maybe Abe left it."

He said it like he wasn't surprised. But I was. Why had Zane stayed with Abe if the man wasn't trustworthy?

"With friends like him, who needs enemies?" I finally asked.

Zane remained stoic.

I drew in a deep breath. "Okay, how about Bianca? Are the two of you dating?" The words left a bad taste in my mouth since it wasn't long ago that Zane had professed his undying love for me.

I didn't really care, but it showed that Zane could be a bit flighty. And flighty wasn't necessarily bad. I'd been accused of being flighty in my life. It was just that once you put everything together, the picture was . . . unflattering, to say the least.

"We're just friends," Zane said.

But were they? So much about Zane seemed sketchy right now. I hated to admit it—either aloud or to myself —but it was true.

"Do you have any idea where Bianca might be?" I asked. "She might have some info that could help us."

"She's probably at Julie's house."

"Julie who?"

"Julie Winders. Bianca likes to crash at her place sometimes. You can probably find her address online."

It was a start, at least. But I still had more digging to do. I leaned back in my hard plastic chair and gripped the phone. "Okay, let me regroup for a minute. Who else could have gotten your gun?"

"Abe is the only person I can think of."

"Why would he sell you out?"

"To take attention off himself, maybe."

I remembered Phoebe's words. Her warning to me about there being a side of Zane I'd never seen before. I didn't want to think it was true, but I also didn't think she would lie to me. I still needed to filter everything he told me right now with that thought in mind.

"Do you have any idea what kind of trouble Morty was up to?"

"No idea."

I sighed, feeling like I was totally on my own here. And that wasn't cool, because this wasn't about me. Zane had asked for my assistance.

Something had to change.

I leaned closer and lowered my voice. "I want to help you, Zane. I really do. But you need to talk to me and tell me the truth. You're being evasive, and I'm one of the only people you have on your side right now."

He dragged his gaze up to meet mine. "Sorry."

An apology was a start. "Zane, why don't you tell me the truth about why you came back here?"

The lines on his face drew deeper. "I went down to South Carolina. I was staying with my friend Benny, and I kept thinking someone was following me. Then these guys confronted me. Said I had something that belonged to them, and if I didn't give it back, they would kill me."

My heartbeat quickened. "What were they talking about?"

"I have no idea. I told them that. But they didn't believe me. They just kept pressing me. Finally, they told me I had a week to find it and get it to them. To prove how serious they were, they shot one of the guys with them."

I gasped. It sounded like something Hollywood would come up with.

"They killed one of their own?" I asked.

He shrugged. "I don't know. Whoever he was, he was on their bad side."

"Did you report this to the police?"

"No, I ran."

I bit back a terse response. "The items they thought you had that belonged to them—could it be the package that Morty tried to give you?" I asked. Were these two incidents connected?

"I don't think so. I have no idea."

I leaned back and shook my head, trying to make sense of what he was telling me. "Why'd you come back here to the Outer Banks, of all places? It seems like you might try to escape them by going somewhere unexpected."

"What better place to escape them than here? I figured that they assumed I would run. So I went to Abe's place and laid low."

"And did you see them anymore?"

"No, but I felt like someone was watching me that night Morty died."

I leaned back, still trying to make sense of everything. "So maybe one of these guys did it?"

"Maybe. I just don't know who they are."

"Do you remember anything about them?" Again, he was giving me so little to go on. How was I supposed to help him?

He shook his head. "No, I'm sorry, Joey. Everything was a blur." He grimaced. "I'm never getting out of here, am I?"

I was still chewing on what Zane had told me when I left the jail and headed back to the police station. Jackson had called and told me everything was ready to go. I couldn't wait to dive in.

Maybe Jackson would even tell me who the Australian woman was.

In the meantime, I kept replaying my conversation with Zane.

He seemed sincere in his words and about his innocence. No matter how many warnings people gave me about Zane and his past, I still wanted to believe the best of him. I wanted to believe he was innocent.

I missed our conversations and adventures. It wasn't until this moment that I realized just how much I'd come to depend on him as a friend, neighbor, and confidant.

I had to figure out who these guys were and what they'd wanted to get from Zane.

Maybe Jackson would open up since he was letting me be the Donkey to his Shrek again. I really needed a new comparison because that sounded stranger every time I thought about it.

I stepped into Jackson's doorway and offered a big, bright grin that showed him how excited I was he'd finally come around to seeing things my way.

"Joey." He straightened some papers on his desk and stood. "You're here, right on time."

I held my chin higher. "Of course. Reporting for duty."

"That's perfect." He moved around his desk and stepped into the hallway. "Because Detective Gardner has been waiting for you."

Confusion rippled inside me. "What?"

His hand circled my arm, and he led me to the hallway, where another detective was waiting. "I know you wanted to tag along so you could see police work in action."

"Right, I wanted to tag along with you—"

Jackson didn't seem to hear me.

"Detective Gardner is covering a very exciting series of break-ins at the public beach parking areas, and that will be followed by a skimmer that was found at a local gas station." Jackson winked. "It sounded exactly like something you would enjoy."

"But—" This was not the way it was supposed to happen.

"The mayor already approved this," Jackson continued. "He loved the idea, for that matter. Maybe Detective Gardner can help you hide some of those rocks."

I crossed my arms and scowled. Jackson had gotten me. Here I thought I'd won, when all along he'd been ahead of me by three steps the whole time.

And now I was stuck.

Jackson winked again, looking entirely too satisfied that he'd figured out a way to appease me and keep me out of trouble at the same time. "You two have fun."

I wanted to argue, but before I could, Detective Gardner turned toward me. "Okay, well, we need to get going. Did you bring your rocks? My kids love finding those things."

Chapter Fifteen

I TWIDDLED MY THUMBS. Car break-ins and skimmers weren't nearly that exciting, and I couldn't even think of any pithy tweets to share.

I couldn't help but wonder what Jackson was doing right now.

He knew something about this case and was trying to keep me away. But what?

Where should I go next for this investigation? I couldn't exactly scope out anyone with a potential Australian accent in the area. With all the tourists around right now, it would be like finding a diamond in the sand.

And the crime Zane had seen? No way was I driving to South Carolina and looking for trouble.

Why was investigating so hard?

"You ready to hide some rocks?" Detective Gardner asked, flicking a Troll doll he had hanging from his rearview mirror.

I'd never really worked with him before, and he was such a happy man. A happy detective. It seemed a little wrong that a detective could be this happy, for that matter.

They should be serious and tough, not overweight and laid back with an affinity for Troll dolls . . . right?

It didn't matter though, because an idea hit me. "Actually, I would love to. I know just the place to start."

"Just give me an address."

I smiled, feeling rather satisfied as I did a quick Google search. A minute later, we were cruising down the road, and we pulled to a stop in front of Julie Winder's house.

"You want to hide them at a residence?" the detective asked. "Isn't it usually in public places?"

"Well, a lot of people pass this house—I mean, area —on their way to the beach. I thought I'd put a couple near mailboxes and stuff."

He shrugged. "I guess that makes sense."

"I'll only be a minute. I'm going to . . . uh . . . talk to the person who lives here first, just to make sure it's okay."

"It's probably a renter."

"You never know."

"Sounds like your problem, not mine. I'm going to start some paperwork, so no hurry."

I grinned again. "Great."

I climbed out and hurried up to the front door of a seventies-style Nags Head cottage. Small, up on stilts, with a screened-in porch at the front. They'd produced these places back in the day like Girl Scout cookies during fundraising season. Like Thin Mints . . . because everyone knew they were the best.

I rang the bell, and guess who answered? Bianca.

And that's Joey for the win.

"Can I help you?" The woman asked before I even said a word.

The same familiar scent of weed wrapped in incense floated out the front door. "I have some questions for you."

"Are you with the city?"

I looked at my jeans and tank top. Did I look like I was with the city? I didn't even have time to address that. "I'm trying to figure out what happened to your ex-boyfriend. I've been looking all over town for you."

"Why do you think I'm here? I don't want to answer any questions." She started to shut the door.

I had to think of something to stop her, and quick. "Did you kill Morty Savage?"

Her lips formed an O. "Of course I didn't. I didn't like him, but that doesn't mean I wanted him dead."

"Who did?"

"I have no idea. I'll say this: he had some kind of new business going with Billy Corbina."

"What kind of new business?"

"I didn't ask for any details. I don't know."

"You have any guesses? Did it have something to do with drugs, by chance?"

"Drugs?" She snorted. "Of course not. Why would you think that?"

I gave her a look, and she frowned.

"Sorry I can't be of any help." She started to shut the door again.

"Any other contacts for this business besides Billy?"

"You could try Evan. That's my best guess. I just don't want anything to do with any messes they've created."

"Just one more question," I pleaded. "Do you know

what might have been in a package he was holding right before he died?"

"No, all I know is that he told me he wasn't going to have to work again a day in his life."

I got home and realized I needed to return the Corvette's keys to Winston Corbina. That thought brought me both a measure of delight and distress.

I wanted the opportunity to chat with him more because I thought he had answers, but I also sensed danger about him. He liked power, and I doubted he let anyone stand in his way. That meant I had to be very careful when I dealt with him.

With a touch of trepidation, I marched to his door and rang the bell. He answered a minute later. I wasn't sure what was going on in his place, but soft music was playing and the lights were dim.

Did he have a woman here with him? Maybe he was having a romantic dinner with someone.

I wasn't going to ask.

He leaned against his doorframe, his hands tucked into the pockets of his super-expensive khakis and way too much chest chair showing from his partially unbuttoned silk shirt.

"How'd you like the ride?" he asked.

I could feel him watching me and trying to read me, and I knew I had to be on guard. "It was great. And the car is still in one piece. As am I."

He smiled, his gaze still too intense for my comfort.

"I should hope so. You might have to make another movie to pay for it, otherwise."

Remind me never to drive a car that expensive again, especially given my track record. "Thanks for letting me use it."

"Anytime."

I glanced beyond him, trying to get a glimpse of who might be with him. Not that I cared. But I guessed I did care just a little. "Well, you sound busy. I should let you go."

"I always have time for you, Joey."

What did that mean? I didn't want to know. Because it almost sounded . . . suggestive.

"Good night," I told him. *More like, good riddance!*

"Good night."

I stepped away when he called my name. I froze, my back muscles tightening as I turned toward him.

"Yes?" My voice cracked.

He was no longer leaning casually against the doorframe. No, he'd straightened and crossed his arms now. "Have you heard anything about your father, Joey?"

Something about the way he asked it made my skin crawl. Was he asking because he thought of my father as a friend? Or for other reasons? I wasn't sure.

"No, I haven't," I said, trying to sound normal. My voice squeaked higher despite my efforts. "Why do you ask?"

"I think about him a lot."

"So do I." Why would he think about my father a lot? Even if I asked, I wouldn't trust his answer. So I didn't even try.

"It's just so strange that he hasn't come back yet, wouldn't you say?"

His gaze latched on to mine again, and I knew he

was searching for the truth. That he wanted to know what I knew.

And I wanted to know what he knew.

And so this silent, unspoken game continued.

"I would say," I finally told him.

He tilted his head, hardly blinking as he watched me. "No idea where he went?"

"I wish I knew."

Tension stretched between us. What was he thinking? What did he know? Why couldn't I shake the truth out of him? Raven Remington would think of a way to get answers . . . but it might include Chinese water-drop torture.

I didn't think it was a good idea for me to try and employ that method. At least not as anything but a last resort.

Finally, Winston nodded. "Take care."

I couldn't help but feel spooked as I walked away.

Chapter Sixteen

JACKSON STOPPED by my place at nine that night, just as he was getting off work. I wanted to ask him what he'd been doing, but I knew he wouldn't answer. And then I'd feel insulted or irritated. So I didn't even bring it up.

Instead, I had a different bone to pick with him. "A string of car break-ins, huh?"

I crossed my arms as we stood near the door, a swath of humidity that had crept in from outside surrounding us—along with a couple of mosquitoes.

It was a good thing for Jackson that I'd just spent the last hour under my grandma's quilt and looking through my dad's old Bible. Otherwise, I might not feel quite so calm and good natured right now.

"I wanted to give you a real-life look into crime in the area." He kept his voice serious, but I could tell by the glimmer in his eyes that he was pleased with himself.

When he squeezed my arm, some of my irritation vanished. Why did he have to have that effect on me? He was in the same category as my grandma's quilt and my dad's Bible.

"Can I get you something to drink?" I needed to occupy myself with something other than wanting to throttle him and kiss him simultaneously.

"No, I'm good."

I sat down on the couch, hoping he'd follow. He did.

I wasn't sure how it happened, but he pulled my feet onto his lap and rested his hand on my calf, as if we'd done this a million times before. We hadn't. But for some reason, it felt natural.

"Am I catching you at a bad time?" he asked.

I wanted to tell Jackson that he could never catch me at a bad time. But then I'd be letting him off the hook too easily. He needed to at least *think* I was still irritated.

"This is as good a time as any," I finally responded.

"I mostly wanted to stop by and check on you. Have you seen Leonard Shepherd anymore?"

I shook my head, realizing that I could at least count that as a blessing. "I haven't."

"Good."

I frowned when I thought about all the crowds I'd been around today. "I suppose it's good. The flip side is that I may not have seen him, but he may have been within sight."

"Let's hope not."

I knew the truth. Jackson wasn't a "hope not" kind of guy. He took precautions. It wouldn't surprise me if he had officers driving past this condo complex every thirty minutes. He'd probably even put out an APB on the guy.

I cleared my throat. "By the way, Zane said someone was murdered in front of him in South Carolina."

"He told me."

Relief flushed through me. "You talked to him?"

"I did a follow-up interview today, and I already talked to the police down there. Nothing has been reported, but they're going to keep their eyes open."

"Good."

I started to sit up some. As I did, Jackson pulled me closer. Instead of saying anything, he wrapped his arms around me and pulled me toward him until my head was nestled under his chin.

"I've been wanting to do this all day," he murmured.

You see? He said things like that, and I just couldn't be mad over the fact that he was keeping professional secrets he'd sworn not to share.

Actually, I supposed I couldn't be mad at him period for being ethical. But still. It was so annoying.

As was the fact that I couldn't kiss him.

Because most of the time, I really wanted to kiss him. I wanted to remember what it felt like to feel his lips against mine. To smell his spicy scent. To feel his gentle stubble against my skin. To feel consumed by something other than my problems.

Before I could relax too much, my phone buzzed.

"I should get that," I muttered.

"Expecting someone?"

"Waiting for a hot date." I winked at him, just to let him know I was joking.

I glanced at the screen and saw I'd gotten a text message from Annette. *I didn't start this page, someone else did. Thought you should know. We'll go live with our own page soon.*

I clicked on the link that was attached, and it took me to a social media page someone had created. It was called #JoeyRocks.

"Hashtag JoeyRocks," I said with a laugh and

showed Jackson on my phone. "There's this whole rock-painting craze—"

"I know."

I stared at him. "You do?"

"Doesn't everyone?"

"I guess I've been hiding under a . . ." I swallowed hard. "A rock."

He chuckled. "That's a good one."

"I try. Tickets are available for my comedy show. It's right here. Right now. You're the only one invited, and you're welcome."

"You're an original, that's for sure."

I continued to scroll through and saw that someone had decided to paint rocks with my hashtag on the back. Whoever the creator of the page was said that each design somehow related to actress Joey Darling.

My interest shifted slightly to concern.

"Look at the front of these rocks, Jackson." I pointed to one that was painted red with little yellow lines and circles on it.

He took my phone and stared at the pictures before shifting uneasily.

Realization dawned on me, and I knew just what he was thinking. "It's my super-stalker fan club. They're handing me clues again, aren't they? Probably something to do with either this current investigation or my father."

His frown deepened. "I'd say that's a great guess."

I leaned back, feeling stunned as I tried to process this. How did this stalker-like fan club of mine get all this information? I could only think of one way: they had people on the inside. But on the inside of what? The Barracudas? The police? Who?

But what would motivate these guys to make it their life work to follow me? Didn't they have jobs? Lives outside of doing this?

I had so many questions, so many things I didn't understand.

But it was time for me to find answers. Maybe I was too much of a lightweight and needed to employ some tougher techniques. Was I really prepared for any of the answers I might find though?

Only if Jackson was by my side. And I had a feeling he wanted me to stay far away from this.

"I can't believe this," I finally muttered, lowering my phone.

"You should just leave these rocks alone and stay far away from these guys. But I know you're not going to do that, are you?"

I glanced up at Jackson, wishing that none of this had ever happened. Wishing this strange fan club had never formed. That I'd never married Eric. That my dad was still here, and that I could just call him up and chat. I wished my life had simply continued on as normal.

But then I would have never met Jackson. Despite everything that had happened—all the hardships I'd faced—I felt my life was so much deeper now that everything I'd held close had been stripped away.

"How can I walk away from this, Jackson?" I honestly wanted to know. I couldn't. I was in too far.

Jackson turned to face me, and his gaze latched on to mine with a ferocious intensity. "Promise me something."

I swallowed hard. "What's that?"

"When you go look for those rocks, you'll take me with you."

The thought of Jackson being at my side made me feel 100 percent better—like I could conquer anything. "I thought you'd never ask."

"Thank you." He ran his thumb against my chin.

But I couldn't get distracted by all the tingles running through my body. "Jackson?"

That mesmerizing look swirled in his eyes as he stared at me. "Yes?"

I swallowed hard, hating to break this moment. But I had something very important to tell him. "I'm going to look for those rocks."

Chapter Seventeen

"WE'VE GOT to figure out where this rock is," I muttered.

Jackson and I almost knocked heads as we looked at the photo on my screen, trying to figure out our next plan of action. Not only was there a picture of the rock, a clue had been left as to where I could find it.

"The number of couples who get married in the Outer Banks each year," I read aloud. "How am I supposed to know that?"

"Google it."

"Well, that sounds awfully simple." But I did it anyway. My eyes widened at the answer. "Twenty thousand?"

"Is that what it says?"

"Yep." I glanced at Jackson. "And even if that's the correct number, how does that help us?"

"What we should be asking is, how is twenty thousand significant to this area?" Jackson said. "Look up twenty thousand plus Outer Banks."

"Really?" Like Google was all knowing or something.

He shrugged. "It's a start."

"Sure thing." I typed it in. My eyes widened when I saw the response. "A restaurant here in the area had a twenty thousand–calorie challenge on Thanksgiving Day. They tried to encourage patrons to eat that much food in one day. The thought of that makes me want to throw up."

"I say we go to that restaurant."

I drew in a deep breath as excitement and fear collided inside me. "I say you're right."

We showed up at Blackbeard's Pleasure, a pirate-themed all-you-could-eat restaurant. It was dark outside, which would make it harder to find this rock. But I didn't want to let this go. Not at all.

While surrounded by the scent of fried shrimp and Old Bay seasoning, I turned on the flashlight on my phone and swept the light over the sidewalk leading toward the front door. Hungry tourists chatted as they waited while heavy-metal music drifted from the inside.

The patrons waiting outside for a late-night meal stared at me very strangely, but I didn't even care.

Even worse—what if someone else found it before I did?

"Mom, look what I found!" a tiny voice announced just as the thought raced through my mind.

I swung my head over and saw a little six- or seven-year-old girl holding up a rock she'd just found in a decorative pirate's chest in the flower bed.

I squinted. It couldn't be. Yet it was.

That was my rock.

I was thirty seconds too late.

"That's great, sweetheart," the mom said, practically ignoring her daughter and staring at her phone instead.

"I've always wanted to find a rock just like this. It's so pretty." The girl—a pretty little brunette with a dirty face and shirt—put the rock under her chin and practically hugged it.

And now it was my turn to ruin this girl's dream. I leaned toward her and talked in the same voice I'd used when I did voice work for *River of Magic*, a Disney cartoon. "Could I see that rock, by chance?"

She pulled it closer to her. "But it's my rock."

"I just want to see it," I continued.

The girl's mom—who looked an awful lot like her daughter with a stain on her shirt and her short curly hair in her face—pulled her gaze away from her phone for long enough to jerk her daughter back, as if I were a kidnapper.

I could just see the headlines on this now. *Joey Darling accused of attempted child abduction.*

Sigh.

"It's my rock!" the girl screamed. "And you can't have it!"

I stepped back.

Okay, obviously this wasn't working.

"Ma'am, I'm with the Nags Head Police, and we believe that rock may be connected with a crime in the area." Jackson flashed his badge. "I'm going to have to ask you to let me see it."

The woman still scowled. "How do I know you're telling the truth?"

Jackson held his badge closer, and an edge of annoyance crept into his voice. "Is this enough proof?"

She studied his badge before frowning. "I suppose. Katy, give this man your rock."

"I don't want to give this man my rock." The child's face turned red.

"It wasn't a request, Katy Ann. It was an order." The mom's voice turned more stern, and she tapped a glittery fingernail against her arm, her patience obviously waning.

Along with mine.

"But I don't wanna. It's my rock. I found it."

You had to be kidding me. What kind of kid got attached to a rock with a weird symbol on it? I might understand if there were a picture of a puppy on it, but there wasn't. It was a gang symbol instead.

"Katy, give him the rock!" The mom's voice was laced with frustration now.

"Here, take it!" Katy flung the rock.

The next thing I knew, I was on the ground . . . and stars were circling my very unstable surroundings.

Chapter Eighteen

"Joey? Can you hear me?" The voice above me seemed to echo and swirl and drift closer before speeding farther away.

The blackness was much easier to embrace. All I had to do was let myself go, and everything wouldn't seem so confusing. The abyss around me was peaceful . . . and sleepiness beckoned for me to come into its folds and rest.

"Joey, talk to me," the voice said again.

I wanted the voice to go away and quit interrupting my quiet time. But the speaker refused to hit Mute.

Against my better wishes, I pulled my eyes open.

The darkness disappeared, replaced with glaring streetlights. The zoom of vehicles in the background. A car alarm whining in the distance. Heavy-metal music in the background.

Slowly, my vision cleared and Jackson's face came into view, as well as a crowd of strangers who stared at me like aliens examining their first human life form. If they tried to probe a needle into my eye, I was going to go redneck crazy on them.

It was in me, buried deep down inside. But it was still there.

"Joey?" Jackson repeated, kneeling beside me. Even through my haziness, I could see the concern on his face.

I tried to remember what had happened, but a throbbing pain in my head made thinking hurt. Yes, it actually hurt.

"I hear you. I think." I rubbed my forehead. "Is this real?"

"This is real," Jackson told me. "The rock hit you square in the forehead."

"Please don't press charges," Katy's mom said above me, wringing her hands together and frowning frantically. "Please."

"Is that Joey Darling?" Someone else took a picture.

The flash caused another round of throbbing through my lobes, and I winced.

Why did these things always happen to me?

"Put the phone away," Jackson growled. "And give the woman some space."

The crowds must have heard the authority in Jackson's voice, because they backed away, thus ending their close encounter of the third kind.

I drew in a deep breath and pushed myself up. My head pounded, and the gravel beneath me dug into my hands. Jackson stretched his arm around me to help me sit up.

"I'm fine. I'm fine," I muttered, both loving and hating that he was fussing over me. "Really."

"We should take you to the hospital." Jackson frowned again and glanced at my hair.

Or maybe it was my forehead. That was throbbing. Could he see it throbbing?

I touched it and felt a huge knot there.

Great.

I was going to look like a mutant polka-dotted unicorn, wasn't I?

Katy's mom gasped. "If you go to the hospital, then you'd have to file a police report, right? My daughter is a good girl. I promise. I don't know why she acted out like that. It's not like her."

I'd bet it was very much like Katy to act like this. But what I really needed was for this woman to be quiet. Her voice was grating on my nerves.

"I'm not pressing any charges," I muttered, touching the knot again and flinching at the shot of pain that rushed through me.

"Oh, thank you. Thank you!" She seemed to think twice and hurried inside the restaurant before I changed my mind.

I didn't even care. I just wanted her gone. And I wanted this headache to go away.

And I needed to know . . . "Did you get the rock, Jackson?"

"Of course that's what you would think of." Jackson reached beside me and grabbed something. "But since you asked, it's right here. I told you this was a bad idea."

"Really? This isn't the best time to prove that you're always right."

He frowned. "Not my most sensitive moment. I apologize. But this has trouble written all over it."

"There you go again." The pounding in my head made me want to scream.

He extended his hand and helped me to my feet. "Is your vision okay? You're not seeing double or anything?"

"No, I don't think so. But have you always had three eyes?"

His eyes narrowed. All three of them. "Are you being funny?"

I flashed a grin. "I'm here all night, folks. Tickets, however, are nonrefundable."

"Still doing the stand-up comedy routine, I see. At least you're acting like yourself." He led me away from the crowd. "There's a message on the back of the rock, Joey."

My silliness disappeared. "What does it say?"

"Look for answers here." He looked back at Black-beard's Pleasure. "I'm not sure what this restaurant has to do with anything that's been going on."

"There's only one way to find out. Let's go in."

He examined my face again. "I'm still worried about your head."

"I'm always worried about my head. That I'm not right in it."

"That could be true." He slipped his arm around me to help keep me steady.

Before we could make another move, a familiar face caught my eye.

It was Leonard Shepherd.

And he was watching us from across the parking lot.

Jackson took off toward Leonard.

I wanted to run also, but I knew I couldn't. I felt too unsteady on my feet, and I knew I'd just get in the way.

I held my breath as I saw Leonard dart onto the busy highway. Cars slammed on brakes. Drivers honked. People yelled things from their windows. I felt as if I was doing a press junket in New York City.

I strained my neck, trying to see what was going on.

Was Jackson okay?

Please let him be okay.

I stepped closer to the hedge of shrubs that separated the parking lot from the street. I desperately wanted a glance. And I wanted answers. And I wanted my head to stop hurting.

Finally, Jackson emerged from the bushes. I darted toward him, pausing only when my head began to spin. He gripped my arms, as if he could sense my unsteadiness.

"What happened?" I rushed, wanting to skip the normal "Are you okay?" questions. If I had a nickel for every time sometime asked me that . . .

"Traffic. He got across and got away before I could catch him."

I frowned, knowing it wouldn't be that easy. "I don't like this."

"Neither do I. Believe me." He examined my face again. "Maybe you should reconsider going to the ER, Joey."

"No, no. I'm fine." It would be a waste of time because the doctor there would tell me the same thing. I knew the drill.

Someone stepped up from behind me—an older gentleman with white hair and glasses. "I saw what happened, and I'm a doctor. If you're not going to be checked out, do you mind if I take a look?"

Jackson and I exchanged a glance, and I finally shrugged. "I guess."

What could it hurt? Maybe it would make Jackson feel better.

The man shined a light in my eyes, studied the knot on my forehead, and asked some questions. Finally he said, "I think you'll be okay, but you need to keep an eye on her." He looked at Jackson. "She can go to sleep, but you need to wake her up every two hours."

"I can do that," Jackson said.

Every two hours? That sounded miserable. But I didn't argue. At least I didn't have to go to the ER. I had other more important things to do.

Things like figuring out why someone had lured me here.

It wasn't just so Leonard Shephard could watch me. There was something here I was supposed to discover. But what?

Jackson and I had to fight our way through a crowd of people waiting to be seated at the all-you-could-eat buffet. We finally reached the hostess, who was decked out in a pirate maiden outfit.

I wanted to tell the people waiting here that all they could eat was a bad, bad choice. But if I were in their shoes, I'd probably be here too. Because all you could eat might be bad for your waistline, but it was oh so tempting for the tummy.

"How many?" Jacklyn Sparrow asked.

Clever name.

Jackson showed the hostess a picture of Morty. "Have you ever seen him before?"

She stared at the picture before responding with a foreign accent. "I just start here. Ask that swab."

She pointed to a busboy in the distance. He was a lanky teen with acne and a name tag reading *Shivering Timbers*.

Jacklyn must be one of the international student workers who came over in the summer to help fill the massive void needed in the job market here. Jumping from five thousand people in town to fifty thousand made it hard to sufficiently fill a lot of jobs.

Jackson cut between tourists with their plates piled high with crab legs and hushpuppies. He reached the boy, showed him his badge, and stopped him in his tracks. "We need to ask you a couple of questions."

"Sure, man."

Jackson flashed Morty's picture. "Seen him?"

"It's Morty. Everyone around here knows him."

"Does he come in here often?"

"Here?" He made a face—drawn chin, squinted eyes, hunched shoulders. "Nah, this place is a tourist trap. No locals come here."

"Has he been in here lately for any reason?" Jackson continued.

He remained quiet and thoughtful for a moment. "Now that you mention it, he might have come in some-time last week."

Bingo!

"What was he doing?" Jackson asked.

"Eating."

Jackson stared down the teenager, who visibly shrank back.

"Sorry. I'd forgotten he came in. Really. I did."

Jackson continued to give the boy the eye. "Was he with anyone?"

He moved his tub of dishes to the other hip. "Yeah, I think he was meeting with someone."

"Anyone you recognized?"

The teen shook his head. "I can't say I did. I don't really remember him. I wasn't paying attention either. It was a busy evening, and I couldn't stop all night. You know how many plates the average tourist eating here goes through per night? Five! And I'm right there, picking up every one of them."

"Do you remember anything about the man Morty was with?" Jackson continued to push.

"No. I'm sorry. I didn't think much of it. Morty and I weren't friends or anything. I just knew him from around town." He paused. "Does this have something to do with his murder?"

"That's what we're trying to find out," Jackson said. "Anyone else who may have noticed something?"

"Nah, not really. The rest of the gang is mostly from Europe or something. Sorry."

Well, we hadn't found out much information. But at least we knew that Morty had met with someone.

It was better than nothing . . . probably.

Chapter Nineteen

WHEN I WALKED into Jackson's house, Ripley greeted me exuberantly—which was to be expected. We'd decided to come here instead of my place, mostly because of Ripley. Besides, this was more secluded and quieter than my condo.

I rubbed Ripley's head, talked in baby babble, and my efforts were returned with doggie kisses to my cheeks and neck.

"Can I get you something to drink?" Jackson asked, dropping his keys on a little table by the front door.

"If I'm going to be up all night, then how about some coffee?" I already dreaded the waking-up-every-two-hours thing and had decided I'd rather stay awake.

"One coffee coming up."

As he made it, I paced around in his living room. I paused by a bookcase and saw a picture there. A sad smile crossed my lips as I stared at it.

It was of Jackson and his deceased wife, Claire. They both grinned from ear to ear in the photo. The sun was perfectly cast in the picture, smearing in the background and adding a warm glow to their faces.

Claire was so beautiful—an all-natural blonde bombshell. Her eyes were warm and full of life—life that had been cut short by the ravages of breast cancer.

I felt Jackson behind me. He didn't say anything.

"You guys looked so happy." Compassion made my voice catch. Divorce had caused a certain kind of grief and loss in my life, but I knew that paled in comparison to losing a spouse to cancer. I couldn't even imagine.

He picked up the picture, and a soft smile captured his lips as he soaked in the image. "We were happy."

I turned around to better face him but was sure to keep everything soft. "What was she like, Jackson?"

I honestly wanted to know. I wanted a glimpse into his past.

He let out a breath and looked at the photo again. His eyes took on a look that I didn't see on him often, it was a mixture of grief, love, and loss. And the sight of it made my heart lurch into my throat.

As tough as Jackson was, there were some burdens hard for the strongest of us to carry.

"She was great," he said. "She was kind of an earth mother. She liked everything organic and natural. She thought the beach could cure anything. She loved fiercely, and if she believed in something, she wouldn't back down."

"She sounds amazing." She reminded me a bit of Phoebe, but I had a feeling Phoebe had been the laid-back sister.

Jackson nodded slowly, thoughtfully. "She was. She would make these pictures out of broken seashells—

she'd put them on pallets and shape them into crabs and lighthouses. She said it was a stress reliever."

"You mean those pictures you have hanging up in the hallway?" I'd noticed them last time I was here.

He nodded.

"I had no idea she made those," I said. "They're beautiful."

"I think so also." He lowered his gaze before setting the picture back on the shelf. "It sounds like the coffee is done. Let me go grab some."

A new kind of somberness washed over me as I went to sit on the couch. I probably should ask him for some Tylenol as well. I didn't want to admit that my head was aching, but it was.

Maybe the caffeine would help.

He brought me a mug. It wasn't a fancy cup, but instead an old beige one that had probably been part of a set at one time—twenty years ago. Silence stretched between us a minute. Not the awkward kind, but the easy kind.

Finally, I tucked a leg beneath me. I'd set a serious tone for the evening, and I wasn't sure if that had been a good idea or not. I decided instead just to go with it.

"So you asked me about my future last night," I started. "Now it's my turn."

"Okay, let me brace myself."

"There's no right or wrong," I promised. "Are you, Jackson Sullivan, ever tempted to move back to the DC area? That's where your family is, right?"

He let out another breath and gripped his coffee. "Maybe at times. But Nags Head has become home. It's worth it to stay, even if it's just for the sunsets and sunrises."

I smiled. "They are pretty amazing here."

Note to self: stop saying amazing.

He turned toward me, examining my face, as he often did. "How about you, Joey? I know I asked you about your future last night, but can you see yourself staying here?"

Oh, he was turning the tables on me. Was I really prepared to answer that question? I didn't know.

"Of course you know why I came to this area," I started, glancing at my coffee mug. Now I was the one who sounded somber. "I need to figure out what happened to my dad. I need to somehow make things right. I never expected to like it so much here."

He stretched his arm across the back of the couch, and his fingers brushed my bicep, sending tingles up my spine.

"I guess the question is, can I be an actress and live here? Am I supposed to keep acting? I mean, I've been given an incredible opportunity and platform. I don't want to take that for granted."

"I agree. You shouldn't. As long as you don't sell your soul for the sake of an opportunity."

"What do you mean?"

"I'm sure it's hard to stay true to your values in Hollywood, Joey. That's all I'm saying."

He hit the nail on the head. "Definitely. I've been there. I've lived that. And I'd like to say I'm stronger now. But what if I'm not? You can train all you want, but until you're doing the marathon, you don't know if your training has paid off."

He brushed my hair from my face. "You can handle it, Joey. You just need a good support system to help keep you accountable."

Support system? Could that be Jackson? Was he offering?

"Another part of me can't imagine leaving you—I mean, this area." I shook my head and my cheeks heated. Had I said that? Had he bought my explanation?

Jackson said nothing.

Speaking of people not telling the truth . . .

"Actually, I mostly mean you." I frowned at my truthfulness, yet I couldn't leave that lie out there. "That was way too honest, wasn't it?"

I might as well have told him I loved him.

I held my breath, half expecting him to run.

Instead, a soft grin lit his face. "Not at all. Thank you. Because I can't imagine you leaving this area for a long time either." His smile faded as he looked around his house. "But could you really see your Hollywood friends coming here for a visit? Seeing you in a little sixteen-hundred-square-foot cottage with a fish-cleaning station downstairs?"

His words caught me off guard. Mostly because I realized that when Jackson dated, he didn't do it casually. He did it thinking of the future. Of marriage. Of forever.

That thought thrilled me and tried to freeze me with fear.

"Jackson, I grew up in a little house with no flower beds and weeds for the lawn," I said. "My dad worked for the railroad, we mostly ate microwave meals, and all my clothes were hand-me-downs. I've never forgotten my beginnings. They've shaped me into who I am today, and I never want to lose that. I've been at places in my life where I've wanted for nothing, and you know what?

I was still miserable. Stuff doesn't make you happy. It's the people in your life that make the difference."

Somehow in the course of this conversation, the two of us had drifted closer together. As in, inches apart.

"Man, do I want to kiss you right now," he said. "I want to forget what I said before."

I smiled. Then I remembered his words. He wanted to make sure I was truly over Eric before we dated. And as much as I hated it, I knew it was a good idea. For a little while longer, at least. Because the more I was with Jackson, the less I thought about Eric. And that was a good thing.

"Well, I know you said you wanted to wait to date me, but who said I wanted to date you?" I teased.

His eyes sparkled, and he pulled me closer. "Are you saying you don't?"

I shrugged, knowing good and well I was giving him a hard time. "I'm just saying that there's an awful lot you're assuming, mister."

"Did you just call me mister?"

I poked him in the stomach with my finger. "Maybe I did."

"You know what I do to people who poke me in the stomach, don't you?"

"What's that?" My nerves tingled with anticipation.

"This." In an instant, he was on his feet.

Somehow my coffee ended up back on the table, and Jackson swooped me into his arms. My arms reached for his neck. He twirled me around, and I howled with laughter.

When he set me back down, my throat clenched. How long could I stop myself from kissing this man? I loved everything about him.

His hand cupped my cheek, and his eyes were mesmerizing as they met mine.

He wanted to kiss me just as much as I wanted to kiss him.

I closed my eyes and relished his touch—leaned into it. I anticipated the feel of his lips against mine. I longed for it more than I longed for air to fill my lungs.

I was in trouble, I realized. Deep, deep trouble. The kind of trouble that developed when your heart took on a mind of its own and you felt powerless to fight it.

Chapter Twenty

THEN A PHONE RANG.

Jackson's phone.

We both tensed. Held our breath.

But I knew what the inevitable was.

He had to answer it.

I opened my eyes and stepped back.

It was probably best that someone interrupted us anyway.

"Excuse me a minute." Jackson stepped away.

As he did, I released my breath, trying to get a grip on my emotions. I sat down on the couch and grabbed a blanket, trying to stop picturing what our almost kiss might have been like.

A few minutes later, Jackson sat beside me.

"Everything okay?" I asked.

"Yeah, it was just about another case we've been working."

"Let me guess: car break-ins and skimmers?"

"It's exciting stuff. Almost as exciting as people

wearing shirts with holes cut in them so they can get polka-dot suntans."

My eyes widened. Had I just heard him correctly? Based on his sparkling eyes, I had. "No they're not."

He raised a hand in Boy Scouts' honor. "I saw two people doing it, and they were talking about you."

My bottom lip dropped. "How did they know? That just happened and . . ."

"Have you checked the rag mags today?"

"I try not to," I admitted. They usually made me mad, which could spiral into something unhealthy.

"Well, I haven't either, but that's my best guess."

I stared at him a moment, my cheeks feeling unusually warm. "So . . . you noticed my polka dots too?"

He made a face—half apologetic, half amused. "It was kind of hard not to."

Yay for that. Or not.

With the moment broken, I leaned back on the couch. I had some other questions that had been pressing on my mind, and now seemed like just as good a time as any to address them.

"Did you check Zane's alibi or the gunshot residue on his hands?"

Jackson nodded slowly. "We did. And I don't know if I'd call it an alibi. Yes, he was at a range practicing his shooting. But that doesn't mean he wasn't also holding the gun when Morty was shot."

I supposed he had a point. "How about Abe? Is he still locked up?"

Again, Jackson slowly nodded. "He is. For a few more days, at least. He's been unable to make bond."

I leaned back and let that sink in. At least Jackson had told me that much. I'd take whatever I could get.

Jackson raised a DVD. "Confession: I secretly like zombie apocalypse shows. You interested in watching some of *The Swimming Dead?*"

I nodded, realizing he was done talking about this. But my thoughts would be dwelling on our conversation for quite a bit longer.

In the middle of a dream where I turned into a polka-dotted unicorn wearing bright-blue eyeshadow, I pulled an eye open with a start.

I squinted with confusion when there were no rainbows in sight.

What a dream.

Where was I?

I started to shift when I remembered last night. I remembered watching TV with Jackson. Trying to stay awake.

But eventually I must have drifted to sleep. Because right now I was in Jackson's arms. Ripley was beside me, his head resting on my leg as he let out little doggy snores.

Jackson and I were both sitting upright on the couch. The TV was still on—the local news was blaring, mentioning something about a storm they were watching out in the Atlantic. My head was snug under Jackson's chin, and I could hear his heart beating against my ear. I could feel his hard chest muscles. I could smell his spicy aftershave.

I probably should have woken him up. But I didn't want to. I wanted to stay here a minute longer.

The thing was this. Although I did have some money

from *Family Secrets* and from a network who'd picked up reruns of *Relentless*, I no longer had a home. I had a ten-year-old car with more than one hundred thousand miles. I had no savings and no retirement, and any money I did have coming in I'd promised to donate to charity. For all intents and purposes, I had nothing.

Yet when I was in Jackson's arms, I felt like I had everything.

And that thought scared the dickens out of me. At the same time, it made me want to hold him tighter and never let go.

I had a bad history of always having to have a man at my side. Of being in love with love. Of dating so I could avoid my problems.

But this felt different. This felt real. And I had no idea what to do about it.

A few minutes later, Jackson began stirring. His voice had a morning huskiness that I could listen to forever.

"Hey." He pushed himself up. "I guess we fell asleep."

"I guess we did."

He glanced at his watch. "And I slept surprisingly well. It's almost eight."

"Is it really?" I hadn't been paying attention.

He ran a hand over his face, then across his head and against his neck. "What do you say we go grab some breakfast somewhere and then head to church?"

"Sounds good. I'll just need to run home and change first."

"I can drive you." He stood and stretched. "Let me just get ready first."

"I'll let Ripley outside," I said. "I'll be downstairs."

With Ripley on my heels, I meandered down the stairs, still reeling from last night. Still extremely tired from staying up for most of the evening. Still dreaming about what it would be like to wake up to Jackson every day.

As soon as I reached the driveway beneath his house, I paused.

I felt someone's gaze on me.

As I glanced across the grass, I saw Crista standing in her yard watering some . . . cacti? Ripley bounded toward her, and she patted his head.

My muscles instantly tensed, and then they tensed again when I realized she wasn't just gazing at me. She was staring—possibly even scowling—at me.

I knew exactly how this looked. And explaining to her that I had a concussion and Jackson had helped me stay awake seemed complicated.

As had explaining my relationship with Jackson. And that was what got me into this whole situation: poor explanations.

To my surprise, Crista charged toward me.

"You could have just told me," she spouted. Her nostrils flared, and her eyes were beady little orbs of accusation.

"This isn't . . . what it looks like." Wasn't that what everyone said?

"Then what is it?"

And here I went. "I was at a restaurant last night, and this little girl threw a rock, and it hit me in the forehead. I had a concussion and—"

"You really expect me to believe that?" She stared at me like I was the village idiot.

I shrugged. "Um . . . yeah. Because it's the truth."

"I heard you guys laughing last night." She said it as if laughing was scandalous.

"We do laugh together a lot. Is that a crime?" I heard the irritation in my voice and decided to regroup. "Look, I wasn't trying to deceive you. Jackson and I like each other, but we're not dating. It's complicated, and I don't feel like I need to explain myself anymore. But I wasn't trying to deceive you."

She nudged her chin up, seeming speechless, if only for a minute.

Before she could say anything, Jackson pounded down the steps. He smiled at Crista as he reached me. Droplets of shower water still clung to his hair, and he'd shaven, revealing smooth, touchable skin. Although I liked his scruff also.

Him looking like this probably only solidified Crista's assumptions.

"Hey, Crista," Jackson said. "Good morning."

Instantly, all her bad vibes disappeared—including her venom-filled eyes and cobra-hood flaring nostrils. "Hey, Jackson. I just came over to say hello. Do you need me to watch Ripley for you today?"

"I'm not sure what's going on today, but I'll be in touch. Would that be okay?"

"Oh, of course. Any time you need me." She waved her fingers in the air and smiled. "Okay, I'll be seeing you around."

What in the world did that interchange mean? Was she still flirting with Jackson? When I said we weren't officially dating, did that mean she felt like she still had a chance?

More frustration pinched at me.

Jackson squeezed my arm. "You ready?"

I nodded, pushing the exchange out of my mind for now. "Let's put Ripley back inside and go."

Chapter Twenty-One

THIRTY MINUTES LATER, Jackson and I sat on a wooden pew in the small, traditional church my father had attended.

I always felt close to my dad when I was in this sanctuary with its beautiful stained-glass windows and glossy wood trim. The connection my dad had with this place was the original reason I'd come here in the first place. I'd wanted to find out anything I could about my dad's last days in this area before he disappeared.

But sitting on this pew took me back in time to my childhood. To my roots. To what was important.

And now I hated to miss a service. I loved the spirit of the people here. The sense of community. The wisdom and reminder of a higher purpose in life.

Halfway through the service, my phone buzzed. It took everything in me not to check it right then and there. But as soon as the last song was sung, I excused myself and checked my messages. Two older ladies caught Jackson and began chatting with him, giving me a moment of privacy.

It was from Annette. Another clue had been posted on the #JoeyRocks page.

I quickly clicked over to see it.

It was another rock with a similar color scheme to the first. The clue that had been left: *Examine the 257*.

What did that mean?

I closed my eyes, tired of these games. Yet I knew I couldn't let this go. I punched in "257 + OuterBanks" into my search engine.

Wouldn't you know, the Cape Hatteras lighthouse just happened to have 257 steps?

"What are you doing?" Jackson asked, joining me.

I showed him my phone screen.

"Another one, huh?"

I nodded. "I don't know about you, but I know where I'm heading."

Jackson and I found the rock hidden in the shadow of the lighthouse. As I examined this second rock, I hoped I might find more answers. But the lines and circles still meant nothing to me, nor did the location.

I glanced up at Jackson, but his expression was hard to read with his sunglasses on.

"What do you think this means?" I asked, stepping into the shade of some live oaks.

He shrugged. "Your guess is as good as mine."

"It obviously has something to do with this investigation," I mused aloud, moving aside so a large group of tourists could get by on the narrow path. "Blackbeard's Pleasure was a location where Morty went last week. Maybe Morty came here also?"

"It's a good guess. But even if he was here, the bigger question is why. What was he up to?"

I glanced around. "We found this near the light-house itself, but there are a lot of hiking trails here, as well as endless amounts of sand dunes. There are a lot of secluded, isolated places."

"Places that are perfect for crimes." Jackson sighed. "Let me see if I can find a park ranger to speak with. I have a couple of friends who work here."

He called someone, and a few minutes later, Ranger Grayson met us. He was in his thirties with dark hair and a beard. He and Jackson did one of those man-hug things.

Before the conversation could start, a strong wind swept across the area, nearly blowing the ranger's hat off.

"Forecasters said that a hurricane might be headed this way," Grayson said, looking up at the branches around us. "It's growing stronger every day, and the red flags are up."

"People still going out in the surf?" Jackson asked.

"Of course. We've already had three rescues this week since the current started to grow stronger. We can't seem to drill it into people's heads that these waters are dangerous." He tugged at his hat again as the wind continued to blow. "But that's not what you came to talk about, is it?"

"Unfortunately, it's not," Jackson said.

"What can I do for you? I assume this isn't a social visit—though I would love to go fishing with you again sometime."

"I wish it was a fun visit." Jackson shifted toward me.

"By the way, I haven't introduced you yet. This is Joey Darling."

I extended my hand and watched as recognition rolled across his features.

"You're the actress I've heard so much about," Grayson said. "My little sister would flip out right now if she knew I was talking to you."

"Would she? That's so sweet. But tell her I'm not really that exciting in real life."

"Are you kidding? And let her down like that?" Grayson swung his head back and forth.

"Joey's life is actually a little bigger than the movies, so don't listen to her," Jackson teased.

Grayson smiled. "She's a huge fan. She's been plotting ways she might run into you even."

"Plot no more," I said. "I'm sure we can arrange something. I'll share my info before we leave."

"That would be awesome." He turned back to Jackson. "There we go getting sidetracked again. What can I do for you?"

"We're following a lead on some suspicious activities that have been going on up in Nags Head." Jackson held up the rock. "It involves these."

Grayson examined it and let out a little grunt. "Never seen it before."

"We suspect this might have something to do with a murder investigation," Jackson explained.

Grayson looked up, curiosity in his gaze. "That body that was found buried in the sand? I heard about that."

"Has there been anything going on around here that's out of the ordinary?" I asked.

"Besides some online 'stars' trying to do stunts on the lighthouse for their YouTube channel?" He sighed.

"We had some reports of some suspicious men meeting in the woods near the Buxton trails."

"What kind of suspicious men?" Jackson asked.

"It's hard to say because we never caught any of them," he said. "They weren't there for long—but long enough for some visitors to spot them."

"Any idea what they were doing?"

"My best guess is a drug deal of some sort. I have no idea why they would meet here as opposed to maybe at their home, where no one would see them. But I don't give these guys advice. Let them do their business out in the open. It's easier to catch them and stop them that way."

"Good to know," Jackson said. "If you discover anything else, would you let me know?"

"No problem."

I smiled at him. "And I'll be in touch."

Jackson was called into work, so I decided to go to Willie Wahoo's. Maybe I could discover something there. I just needed to stay on the down low, I reminded myself as I walked inside.

"If it isn't Joey Darling?"

"Hey, Joey, my girl."

"Can I have your autograph?"

Okay, so maybe Willie Wahoo's on the down low wouldn't be happening this afternoon. Wouldn't you know that this just so happened to be the one day that I knew several people who were hanging out there?

I smiled, trying to be gracious, and then I sat at the bar and ordered seltzer water with cucumber and mint.

I didn't do alcohol, mostly because it made me into someone I didn't want to be. I hadn't touched the stuff in more than a year.

At once, memories of being here with Zane flooded my thoughts. He was my first friend when I arrived in town. He'd tagged along on my first case and had brought me to this very place in a quest for answers.

I smiled as I remembered him pulling me up onto the bar so we could sing karaoke to "Summer Loving" from *Grease*. It had been fun and freeing and had solidified our friendship. Then he'd kissed me, and confusion had set in. Despite that, we'd pressed on as friends. He'd even gone to LA with me for my *Family Secrets* movie premiere.

Now he was behind bars and accused of murder. I was surprised the *National Instigator* hadn't caught wind of it. Or maybe they had. I wasn't going to check.

I pressed my lips together. This wasn't the way I wanted things to turn out. I wanted a happy ending, but that was seeming less likely all the time.

I closed my eyes a minute and listened to "Total Eclipse of the Heart" playing on the overhead. I listened to the chatter of patrons. At the click of wood hitting balls on the pool table.

Once I felt like my mind was more focused, I forced my eyes open, determined not to waste a single opportunity.

My gaze drifted around the restaurant. Billy Corbina was behind the bar. He was about my age, with a shaved head that sported a scar of some sort at his temple. He thought he was all that and a bag of . . . well, chips seemed too tame. A bag of "I'm special" cards.

I watched him, interested in seeing if he acted like he was in mourning. From what I could tell, he was acting the same—unfazed by the tragedy one of his friends had endured. He laughed. Served alcohol. Winked at a pretty girl who passed.

Wasn't that interesting?

I watched as a man I'd never seen before—that was nothing unusual, especially considering it was tourist season—walked over to Billy. The two chatted, leaning their heads close.

Interesting.

The other man looked sketchy. I mean, I tried not to judge and everything. But when you were tatted up and down your arms and neck, when you sagged your jeans, and when you had a shady gaze, people drew conclusions.

I made a mental note of the man, just in case I needed to reference him later. Could he possibly be the man Morty had met with at Blackbeard's Pleasure?

"Didn't anyone ever tell you it's not polite to stare?" I looked over and saw Morty's friend Evan slide up beside me.

"It's a free country," I finally said. It seemed lame, like a line from TV. Actually, it was a line from television. "Who's the guy Billy is talking to?"

His face went a little paler, and he shrugged. "Beats me."

I didn't believe him.

"Weren't you friends with Morty?" I continued.

He shrugged again. "Maybe."

"I'm sorry for your loss."

"Yeah, I am too. He was a good guy. He had some problems, but don't we all?"

"What do you think happened?" It was amazing the answers I got when I asked that simple question.

"I don't know. And if you're smart, you'll stop asking that question."

It wasn't the response I'd hoped for. "I'm surprised you're not the one out there asking questions. You were his friend."

"I know who you are." He scowled and downed another gulp of his beer. "You're Zane's friend."

"You know Zane?"

"Of course I know Zane. We all hang together."

"Do you think he did it?" I asked.

He snorted. "Beats me. Not really. But do you ever really know people?"

I turned toward him. "What was in the package Morty tried to give Zane before he died?"

His face grew even paler. "What package?"

"You know the package I'm talking about."

He glanced at Billy and rubbed his throat. "No, I don't."

He was spooked. But why?

Billy glanced at his watch. "I've got to go. I've got a meeting I can't miss."

Billy was leaving? During prime business hours? That seemed unlike him. Just who was he meeting?

Billy grabbed his keys and started toward the back exit.

This conversation was getting me nowhere. But maybe following Billy would.

Chapter Twenty-Two

I'D FOLLOWED BILLY, hoping to get some type of clue. Instead, I discovered what kind of grocery store he liked to shop at. I'd given up after thirty minutes.

It was just as well because I'd totally forgotten that I'd told Dizzy we could have coffee together today. We met at my favorite joint, Sunrise Coffee Co., and I told her about my day thus far, ending with my conversation with Evan and me following Billy.

"We should go to Billy's house," Dizzy said. "It seems like the only obvious thing."

"I don't even know where he lives." I'd gone to a party he'd hosted once, but I was pretty sure he'd rented that beachfront mansion just for the occasion.

"I do."

I stared at her. "How do you know that?"

"Because I cut his housekeeper's hair. She told me." She paused. "You want me to bring the Hot Chicks?"

I shook my head. I wasn't even sure I wanted to bring Dizzy. I loved her, but the woman was like a heat-seeking missile when it came to drawing attention to herself.

"No, just you and me would be great."

She stood. "Let's go then."

"Um . . . okay then." I was used to being the one with the foolhardy, impulsive ideas. Being pressured into doing something dumb by someone else left me feeling off balance.

A few minutes later, we were in my car, and Dizzy was staring at her phone and spouting out directions. Several turns later, we pulled up to a house in the Colington community of the Outer Banks. According to Dizzy, mostly locals lived in this area since it was off the beaten path from the ocean.

I parked on the street, several spaces down from Billy's place. The sky had grown dark—partly because it was getting late and partly because we were supposed to have thunderstorms anytime now. The wind had already picked up, sending stray leaves running for their lives across the asphalt.

Which was exactly what Dizzy and I should be doing also.

I'd seen a car in the driveway as I passed, and I knew it was Billy's. He was here. So now what did we do? Staring at the car and house didn't seem productive.

"Let's go see what he's doing." Dizzy opened the car door.

"Wait, wait, wait." I grabbed her arm. Was this what Jackson felt like with me all the time? God bless his soul for putting up with this and not wringing my neck. "What are we going to do? The house is on stilts. We can't even peek inside."

She nodded at the foliage surrounding the place.

154

"But it's got some nice-sized trees around it. You can just climb one of those."

"Oh, I can just climb one, huh? That sounds . . . productive." And dangerous. Especially with my track record for accidents.

"You did that one time on *Relentless*."

"Correction: *Raven* did it on *Relentless*. I was actually sitting three feet from the ground, but special effects are a wonderful thing."

"You can do it."

If only everyone had that much confidence in me.

"Okay, let's give this the old college try." I climbed out, resigned to the fact that I had no better ideas.

Staying out of sight was going to be difficult considering that Dizzy was wearing a bright-purple caftan that would look close to an orb out in the woods. But at least it was getting darker. As long as it didn't start lightning and the bolts didn't illuminate us, maybe we could remain hidden.

Dizzy made cute little high-pitched sounds as we walked through the foliage. *Oh. Oops. Wow. Ouch.* That woman could be a cartoon character. And that was one more reason I loved her.

Finally, we reached the side of the house.

I'd imagined Billy living somewhere else. Somewhere more high class and central to beach life. He was the kind of guy who liked his social status, who wanted people to envy him.

So why had he chosen such a secluded location?

Privacy, I realized.

"See what he's doing!" Dizzy said.

"I don't even know where he is in the house." My

anxiety crept higher and higher up my spine, stopping and leaving me with a tight neck.

Just then, a light popped on in one of the windows.

"It's a sign," Dizzy said. Then she pressed against a tree and shook it like coconuts might fall down. "This is a good climbing tree."

"What if he's changing clothes?" I argued.

"Then you get a show."

"I don't want a show." Especially not from Billy. Gross. And inappropriate. Shame on Dizzy.

"You'll never know unless you look."

I sighed. It was a good thing I'd been a tomboy when I was younger. But it had been a long time since I'd put my tree-climbing skills to the test. I supposed now was just as good a time as ever. And live oaks *were* awesome climbing trees.

I pulled myself up to the first branch and then glanced around for where to go next. Everything came back to me pretty easily. Without much effort, I reached near the top of the tree.

As I paused, the wind blew and the entire tree swayed back and forth. A drop of rain hit my cheek. I waited, expecting more precipitation, but none came. The downpour was going to hold off for a little while longer, it appeared.

I paused near the window. Before I looked inside, I glanced down.

Dizzy gave me a thumbs-up.

But that wasn't really what I noticed.

Mostly I took note of the fact that I was super high up. And then I remembered that my problem had never really been going up. It had always been going down. Heights sometime made my head spin.

All I needed was another knot on my head. I wouldn't be a unicorn then. I'd be a horned creature from a horror movie.

I quickly looked back up. As I did, I spotted Billy.

Thankfully, he had his clothes on. He was sitting at his desk, typing on his computer.

I ducked so the branches and leaves would conceal me. And then I watched.

My heart raced as I saw a woman slide up beside Billy. She was a thin brunette with tattoos covering an arm and a pierced nose. She wore khakis and a black T-shirt.

Billy pointed to the computer screen.

Thanks to a cracked window, I could just barely hear their words and . . . my heart skipped a beat.

She had an Australian accent!

"Everything is going according to plan," Billy muttered, turning toward her. His voice almost sounded like a growl. "Don't blow it."

The woman flinched and backed up.

I held my breath. I hated it when men spoke to women in those tones. Like *hated* it hated it. I wanted to reach through the window and smack some sense into him.

"I won't." The woman frowned. "But what about Currie?"

"I'll handle him."

She wasn't the type to stand up to Billy, I noted. She kept her gaze lowered, and her entire body looked tense.

What exactly was their relationship? I couldn't get a good read on it.

"This has to happen Tuesday night," Billy said.

I leaned closer.

What had to happen? Was this the information I'd been searching for?

The woman said something I couldn't make out.

I crept out farther on the branch. I could feel that this was my opportunity to get the lead I was looking for. If I could just get a little closer . . .

"You know the location," Billy said.

I held my breath and leaned in, waiting for a long-anticipated clue.

As I did, the branch broke.

And I toppled toward the ground.

Chapter Twenty-Three

Dizzy moved entirely faster than I thought possible.

She plucked me up like a hungry diner forking some fried chicken from atop a salad made from broken branches, leaves, and grass. I was in the woods and out of sight in five seconds flat.

My body ached everywhere, I may have had some cuts, and my ego was majorly bruised. But none of that was as important as remaining concealed from Billy.

Billy and the mystery woman stared at the carnage of my life . . . I mean, of my fall.

"It must have been this branch that made the commotion." Billy glanced into the woods, gripping a gun in his hand. "I wonder what caused it to break."

I ducked again, praying he didn't see me or purple-orb Dizzy. If her dress didn't draw his attention, her bright-blue eyeshadow probably would. It could very well look like mini-lightning strikes in the distance.

"Must have been the wind," the Aussie woman said, staring at the ground. "A storm is coming in."

"Must have been." Billy scanned the landscape one

more time. Finally, he turned back to his friend. "Okay, come on. Let's go. We've got a lot of work to do."

They climbed into the car a few minutes later and pulled away.

It was only then that I allowed myself to feel. To think. To process.

"Are you okay?" Dizzy rushed, looking at me and frowning. "All I could think was that Billy was going to kill you if he found you. I figured it was better I further damage a broken arm or a broken butt bone than to let Billy find you."

Speaking of a broken butt bone . . . I rubbed mine. It was achy. Could you really break a butt bone? "I guess I should thank you."

"Who would have thought that branch would have broken?"

"Yeah, who would have thought?" I felt my elbow. The back of my head. My knee. My heinie again. Everything appeared intact. I didn't even see any cuts. I couldn't believe it.

"Did you hear anything?" Dizzy asked, her concern over me now an afterthought.

"Billy and that lady are planning to meet someone on Tuesday. I couldn't hear who or where or why. Maybe some guy named Currie. I climbed out as far as I did, hoping to hear more. But it was all for nothing."

"Oh man. That's too bad. That information would have been helpful." She frowned and snapped her fingers in an *oh shucks* motion.

"Tell me about it." I puckered my lips in a half pout. Had all this been for nothing?

"So what are we going to do now?"

I did a double take at her. "We?"

"I'm in this with you now."

That could only spell trouble.

As she said the words, the sky opened and rain began pouring down.

I knew I should run to my car and get out of here. But I felt like I was so close to answers. I wasn't ready to leave yet.

"I need to see if his door is unlocked," I muttered.

Dizzy's eyes lit with excitement. "I'll let my hair go for this."

I knew she was serious if she offered to sacrifice her hair.

We ran through the woods to the back of the house and ducked under the covered driveway there.

It was a long shot that anything would be left open and we'd be able to get inside. But it wasn't unheard of for people to leave their doors unlocked around here. And Billy had left in a hurry, so maybe there was hope.

I climbed the stairs to a landing beside one of the outside doors and twisted the handle. It didn't budge.

"We tried," I told Dizzy, hurrying down the stairs before anyone could see me. It had been a bad idea, and this was God's way of keeping me out of trouble.

"There are other doors," she reminded me.

I supposed there were. I was going to start calling her Dizzy the Militant. She really *was* a drill sergeant.

I paused and looked around. There was another stairway beneath the house.

"I'll try one more door," I said. "And then I'm out of here!"

She shimmied with excitement. Why wasn't this woman more nervous? Had she been a cat burglar in a past life? I was beginning to think so.

I darted up the other set of stairs.

This door would be locked. Certainly. Billy was too smart to leave it open.

I rubbed my hands together with nervous energy and reached for the handle . . . and wouldn't you know, the door opened?

My heart stuttered a beat. I just couldn't catch a break, could I? Unless it was a tree branch. But they didn't count.

The door was unlocked, so I had no excuse not to go inside. Except for the law. And fear of being arrested. And . . . well, a million other reasons.

I sighed and turned, nearly falling over when I saw Dizzy beside me. When had she joined me?

She squealed with delight. "I can't believe our luck!"

She probably thought she was living out an episode of *Relentless*. Some people had trouble separating fiction from reality. I'd always suspected Dizzy fell into that category, and this outing was proving it.

"I can't believe it either," I muttered.

Nor could I believe I was about to break into Billy Corbina's home. If he caught me here . . . I shuddered. I couldn't even think about what he'd do. Fillet me and feed me to the fish, probably.

The man had a very dark side.

I stepped inside, and my insides pinched tighter with anxiety. You'd think I was an amateur at this. Sadly, I wasn't. I was the one who was becoming a professional at these things, not Dizzy. How many homes had I sneaked into since I'd moved to this area?

I'd lost count.

I just needed to move, I realized.

After drawing in a deep breath, I ventured deeper

into Billy's lair. I didn't pay attention to anything I passed. I didn't have time. Instead, I went directly to the room where I'd spotted Billy from my perch outside.

I paused and gathered my surroundings. There was a bed on one wall. A dresser. Some perfume sat on top. Eau de Sunset.

None of that mattered.

I rushed toward his desk and began rummaging through the papers. There was a drawing there. Almost like a blueprint. What was this? I had no idea.

Just in case it was important, I took a picture.

One other paper caught my eye. There were names —they looked like last names maybe. Beside the names were numbers.

What did the numerals mean? I had no idea.

I took a picture of them also.

Out of curiosity, I hit a key on his computer. The screen lit. I tried various passwords, but nothing worked. Of course.

What had I learned by being here? I wasn't sure. Maybe nothing. Maybe something. All I knew right now was that I needed to get out of here.

———

I didn't breathe easily until Dizzy and I were back in my car. We'd survived. And I was pretty sure Billy would have no idea I'd been in his place. I'd left everything as I found it.

The bad news was that it had started pouring rain. No sooner had we locked our doors did Dizzy's phone ring. Winona informed her that Beach Combers had sprung a leak.

I took Dizzy there to check things out. It was apparent a bucket beneath the leak wasn't going to cut it. Water had already saturated one wall, and a steady stream was falling over the reception area.

Dizzy sent me to the store to get a few supplies to patch things up until she could get a contractor out.

Forty minutes later I left the store with her list checked off. It wasn't what I wanted to be doing necessarily, but I couldn't leave her hanging.

I sighed when a cop car pulled up beside me in the parking lot. Jackson. He rolled down his window, and I rolled down mine.

I could tell this wasn't a casual or accidental visit. He'd found me here for a reason.

"Well, hello, officer," I said in a playfully sultry voice. I batted my eyelashes and rested a hand beneath my chin.

"You are not one of those women, Joey." A grin curled his lip.

I was sure many women had taken one look at Jackson and tried to use all their charm and good looks to both get out of any tickets and to get Jackson's attention.

I dropped my act. "Please tell me you're not one of those cops. The tough ones just looking for something to ease their boredom."

"Joey, I hate to ask you this, but what's in that bag?" He nodded toward the bag in the seat beside me.

I held up the paper bag with my purchases, certain I hadn't heard correctly. "In here?"

"Yep, that's the one."

"Just a few things Dizzy asked me to pick up."

"Like what?"

"Clorox, duct tape, and a tarp. Why?" Seriously, why was this conversation even happening?

The twinkle in his eyes grew brighter. "The clerk at the store just called the police station to report you."

"Why would he report me? What sense does that make?" Sure, the man had looked like Grizzly Adams, and he'd stared at me strangely the whole time I was inside. But I'd thought it might be because he kind of recognized me.

A minor sense of outrage rushed through me. Hadn't the man ever heard of privacy?

Jackson shrugged, looking mildly entertained. "Oh, I don't know. Maybe he thought you were about to clean up a crime scene and dispose of a dead body."

"What? All because I bought——" And then it hit me exactly what I'd purchased. "It's just a coincidence."

The corner of his lip twitched. "Would you mind sharing why you bought those things?"

I sighed. "Dizzy had a water leak at Beach Combers. I'm helping her protect all her equipment by wrapping it with a tarp and duct tape. Clorox is a preventive measure for mold, she said."

Now that I said it out loud, it did sound suspicious, didn't it?

Jackson burst into laughter and ran a hand over his face. "Oh, Joey, Joey, Joey. The strangest part about this is that you're serious."

I shrugged and leaned back in my seat. "What can I say? I live a strange life."

"I'd say." His laughter faded, and he shook his head as if still perplexed by me. "Do you guys need help?"

I shook my head. "No, I don't think so. Dizzy is viewing this as an adventure."

"That's a good way to look at it, I suppose. Everything else going okay?"

Should I tell him about what happened at Billy's? The information I'd seen? The woman he'd been with?

I'd only end up with a lecture about how unwise my choices had been.

Not now, I decided. I needed to think this through more. I needed more hard evidence first.

"Pretty uneventful," I said instead.

"By the way, you have a leaf in your hair."

I reached up, pulled it out, and shrugged. "What can I say? It's a new fashion statement."

Chapter Twenty-Four

I GOT BACK to my place that evening after I finished helping Dizzy cover everything inside Beach Combers with a tarp and duct tape. A contractor was coming tomorrow, and he'd give Dizzy a better idea of what needed to be done.

In the quiet of the condo, I sat on my bed with a piece of paper to try and sort out my thoughts. I jotted down what I knew so far. It was kind of like reviewing a script. I needed to see it, to read the words, to study them, in order for everything to sink in.

Morty was dead. Shot in the chest. Buried in the sand beneath a beachside mansion.

Zane was arrested. Kevin James had seen him arguing with Morty. Zane's gun was used in the crime. Gunpowder residue was on his hands, and cocaine was found in his room at Abe's place.

Zane also thought he saw a murder occur while in South Carolina, so he ran for his life and came back to this area earlier than planned.

That whole progression and story still perplexed me.

Why had Zane come back here and moved in with Abe of all people? There was something I was missing.

Bianca broke up with Morty. Was there more to that story? Did that woman know something she wasn't telling me? Were Bianca and Zane having a fling?

Billy and Morty may have been doing some kind of business together. Drugs maybe. Could that possibly be the root of all this?

Morty met with someone at Blackbeard's Pleasure, which could be significant because a rock had been left there. I had no idea who or what the significance would be.

Morty also possibly met with someone at Hatteras Lighthouse, and I also still had no clue who or why.

Annette heard Evan and Morty talking late at night with a woman with an Australian accent.

Billy met with someone with an Australian accent at his home.

Random names and numbers were written on a paper by Billy's computer, as well as some kind of blueprint that made no sense.

I sighed and leaned back. Was I missing anything? How did these pieces connect?

Drugs were the only thing that made sense. Morty and Billy were selling cocaine, and the Australian woman was helping them, but something went terribly wrong. Morty died as a result.

Had he tried to take off with some money? To strike out on his own? What was in that box he tried to give to Zane?

I rubbed my head, the questions making my temples throb. I pressed on, nonetheless.

Then there were the rocks. The strange lines and dots on them. The locations.

I'd bet Leonard had left them. What was he trying to tell me? Was he dangerous?

I had so many questions, and I didn't even know where to start.

I sighed and put the paper down on my nightstand.

Maybe the best place to start was with some sleep.

The next day, I still wasn't sure what I should do or where to go or whom to talk to.

Raven Remington always seemed to instinctively know her next step. In real life, investigating wasn't that easy. For me, at least.

I spent the morning in my condo talking to Rutherford on the phone. Talks were progressing nicely for *Relentless* to be picked up for Netflix. He also sent me a couple of other movie scripts that he thought had promise, and I told him I would look at them.

I agreed to a couple of interviews and promised to review an endorsement deal.

"What's going on with this new suntan tattoo thing?" he asked during a break in conversation.

I froze on the couch where I'd been sitting with my coffee and my favorite quilt. "What are you talking about?"

"There was something in the *Instigator* about how you wore a special shirt that gave your skin polka dots. Now people are selling shirts with designs cut out and calling them suntan tattoos."

I grimaced. Dermatologists from across the country

were going to curse me. I self-consciously rubbed my arm, where I knew one of those circles was mocking me right now. "Interesting."

A moment of silence fell, and then Rutherford got to the real heart of the matter. "When are you coming back to Hollywood, Joey?"

His question instantly made me feel twenty pounds heavier—twenty pounds more burdened, for that matter. I pressed myself harder into my couch, wishing I could disappear into the soft cushions.

"I don't know. Maybe I won't come back." My throat lost all its moisture as I said the words.

"Now you're talking ridiculous. If you want a career, you have to come back."

"Plenty of actors and actresses live away from tinsel town," I said.

"No successful ones."

"Demi Moore." *Ha! Take that, Rutherford!*

"When was she in a movie last?"

I tried to remember but couldn't. *Daggonit!*

"You need to think long and hard about your career, Joey. This is a make-or-break moment for you. Don't let some small-town detective ruin a promising future."

I took total offense to what he said—offense as in I wanted to reach across the phone line and smack him. Instead I squeezed the handle of my coffee mug so hard I feared it might snap and took a deep breath.

"Being famous isn't the pinnacle of life."

"And love is?" He snorted. "Love will let you down, Joey."

"Spoken like someone who's been married three times." I probably shouldn't have said that, but it was the truth. I was going to call Rutherford out if he tried to play mind games with me.

"Touché. Careful or you'll follow in my shoes."

Heat burned my cheeks.

I didn't appreciate his insinuation. I'd wanted to get married only once. I had no idea the man I'd fallen in love with—Eric Lauderdale—would turn out to be abusive. I'd let myself down when I'd gotten divorced, but our marriage couldn't be fixed. Not if I wanted to survive.

I decided not to acknowledge his implication. "Hollywood can also let you down. It's more fickle than love."

"I can't deny that." Rutherford's voice sounded wry and hoarse with cynicism. "But I do think you should think long and hard, Joey. There's no turning back time."

I hung up, and melancholy washed over me.

Being here in the Outer Banks had been fun. Being with Jackson was fun. More than fun. He was unlike anyone I'd ever met before, and he did crazy things to my heart.

But what would I do when I found my dad— because I was determined I *would* find my dad, if it was the last thing I did.

I couldn't stay here and cut hair for the rest of my life. Well, I could, but would that really satisfy me? I didn't think so.

And right now I could live off the money I made on my previous body of work. But I knew that cash wouldn't last forever. Even if I were super frugal—something I wasn't known for being—eventually those paychecks would run out.

I sighed, closed my eyes, and let my head drop back into the couch.

I didn't really want to think that hard about the future. I'd rather just enjoy the moment. But at some point, I would need a wake-up call.

Until then, I would focus on finding my dad. Every mystery I solved in the meantime helped me to learn the ropes.

Just as that thought entered my mind, my phone buzzed. It was a message from Annette.

There had been another rock drop.

Chapter Twenty-Five

I STARED at the computer screen at the #JoeyRocks page, trying to interpret what the picture and clue might mean.

The clue said *2310*. That was the clue. What was that number directing me to? I had no idea. An address?

My extensive Google-utilizing skills did no good. No one would ever mistake me for Tony Stark—for more than one reason.

That rock was somewhere. And maybe it was the final clue I needed to put these pieces together.

I did the only thing I could think of. I called Jackson and told him the update.

"Does that number make any sense to you?" I crossed my fingers.

"It does," he said.

I waited for him to continue, but after a few seconds, I wasn't sure he would.

Finally, he sighed. "I'm going to tell you, but only because I know you'll figure it out later anyway. Joey, that's the address where Morty was found."

My pulse spiked. "Good to know."

"Don't go there alone, Joey."

"But—"

"I'll pick you up."

I smiled, thrilled that he hadn't asked me to stay away. "It's a deal. I'll see you soon!"

True to his word, Jackson picked me up ten minutes later, and we went to the scene of the crime. As I walked between the houses on the path leading to the ocean, I remembered being here on Friday. I remembered the horror of realizing it was Morty's dead body.

I paused for a moment at the crest of the dune, and a cool wind blew across my face. There was definitely a storm brewing out to sea. If the weather forecasters had their predictions right, it was going to be a big one. However, they expected it to stay out in the ocean and not come ashore.

"Anything new?" Jackson asked as we continued toward the beach.

Again it pressed on me that I should tell him about my nosiness and breaking in to Billy's place. But I knew he'd be disappointed. Probably lecture me. Until I knew if what I'd found was significant, I didn't want to deal with that.

I wasn't sure if that choice was wise or not. But I was going to hold on to my resolve for now.

"Nope, not really." Just then, I spotted something near a post, partially concealed by the dune grass.

It was the #JoeyRocks gift that my stalker had left for me. Jackson picked it up, careful to hold it with a plastic bag—just in case there were prints. I leaned closer for a better look.

Another set of lines and dots were painted across the surface.

"This is one of the strangest things I've seen in all my years of detective work," Jackson said.

"Someone is trying to tell me this location is important. Just like Blackbeard's Pleasure and the Hatteras Lighthouse."

"But why are they important? How does this fit with Morty?"

At least Jackson and I were asking the same questions.

Just then, movement caught my eye.

Someone was behind some sea oats, crouched low as if he or she wanted to remain hidden.

It was Leonard Shepherd.

Again.

Jackson saw him at the same time I did.

"He's not going to get away this time," he muttered.

And then Jackson took off after him.

This time Jackson tackled Leonard on the sand. He dragged him to his feet and snapped some handcuffs on his wrists.

I hurried to catch up with them, not even caring about the onlookers. There were plenty of them staring at the spectacle being played out here at the beach.

"Are they shooting a new scene for *Relentless*?" I heard someone murmur in the distance.

I could see where someone might think that.

But this was all too real.

My heart pounded with anticipation. With a thirst

for answers—a thirst that had been growing in me for a long, long time.

I studied Leonard's face as I approached. It was partly covered with sand from Jackson's tackle. His hair and his scruffy beard matched the sand. His skin was slightly greasy, and even though the man was in his fifties, he still had a few zits. He was scrawny and probably five eight. Something about him just looked squirrely and untrustworthy.

"Why have you been following me?" I asked.

His eyes widened when he saw me, not with fear but with admiration—or something he mistook for admiration. Obsession maybe?

"Because I love you, Joey." He licked his lips. "I've always loved you."

Cold fear dripped down my spine. "You don't know me."

Jackson kept a grip on Leonard's bicep, pulling him back before Leonard could even think about stepping closer.

"I saved your life, Joey. I could have died."

I remembered that day. He was telling the truth. The man had distracted a killer before the guy could finish me off. And then he'd disappeared and continued stalking me.

"And I appreciate that," I told him, shoving a hair out of my eyes as the wind blew against me. "But you've also scared me beyond measure."

"I only wanted to watch out for you." His eyes looked so earnest—but did something else linger there? Malice maybe? Some kind of sign that something wasn't right?

Jackson turned to address him, his jaw hard. "Why are you leaving these rocks?"

Leonard's demeanor changed as he looked at Jackson. "That's noneya. None of ya business."

Jackson glowered at him. "I don't think you know who you're talking to."

"You're the man who thinks you can steal Joey from me."

"Steal Joey from—" I started.

Jackson cut me off. "You know something about what's going on here. You need to tell us what."

"If I wanted to tell you, I would have. I left you the clues to figure everything out."

"How do you know anything?" Jackson asked.

"There are advantages to being the guy that no one ever sees," Leonard said. "No one notices a scrawny, middle-aged man like me. I blend right in."

"Do you know who killed Morty?" Jackson continued.

"Figure out the clues I left you."

Jackson let out a breath, obviously trying to control himself. Then he backed up and pulled out his phone. "I'm calling someone to take you down to the station."

"You can take me." Leonard's eyes were on me, not Jackson.

"I don't want you in the same car with Joey." He put the phone to his ear and called someone.

But I still had questions.

I implored Leonard with my eyes, desperate to know the truth. "Leonard, I know you've been watching me. Who are these other people who are helping you? What do you know about them? Please tell me."

A smug look crossed his face. "They all like you. But not as much as me."

"Who are they?"

He shrugged. "I don't know any names. I know one is a cop. One's a journalist. Another one claims to be your friend."

My friend? My unease grew by the minute.

"What else do you know, Leonard?" I asked. "You're the only one with answers."

Yes, I was imploring to his pride. I didn't even care if he took it the wrong way. I was so close to learning the truth.

The smugness deepened but intermingled with a look of curiosity. "You don't know, do you?"

"Know what?" Seriously, I had no idea.

He leaned toward me. Jackson kept a hand on him and listened carefully to our conversation.

"Someone put a bounty on you," Leonard said.

Chapter Twenty-Six

MY HEART THUDDED a beat as Leonard's words echoed in my ears. This whole conversation felt surreal, like a nightmare I should wake up from. "What does that mean?"

"Someone is paying out rewards to anyone who posts information about you, what you're doing, where you're going. Any aspect of your life, really."

Everything else faded until I could only hear my heart pounding hard in my ears. "Why would someone do that?"

There were many things I'd expected him to say, but never that. It made no sense. Or I didn't want it to make sense.

Leonard shrugged. "It's a game. Like hunting. Some guys need a bigger rush, so they head to Africa for their lions and elephants. Others get a little more creative and keep things closer to home."

"Who's paying the bounties?" Jackson demanded, his grip visibly tightening on Leonard's arm.

Leonard shrugged. "I have no idea. I'm only a participant."

"What's the payout?" Jackson asked, his voice deeper than usual. It was his no-nonsense tone, and I always cringed when he used it on me.

"Five thousand for good details."

Five thousand? That was no small amount. And it was so unbelievable that someone would do that. It seemed . . . extreme. Dramatic. Sad.

"How much have you 'earned' so far?" My throat was dry and achy as I asked the question. I crossed my arms, trying to ward away the wind, but my hair was blowing in my face and irritating me. But not as much as Leonard was irritating me.

"Twenty thousand. It's quite lucrative."

Twenty thousand? And he was just one participant. Who would have the money to do something like that?

Only one person came to mind.

Winston Corbina.

Could he be behind this?

I wasn't sure. But I didn't like the thought of it.

Another officer picked up Leonard Shepherd to take him to the station. As they drove away, Jackson remained there on the beach, seemingly in no hurry. His jaw was set with determination, and I could tell that whole conversation had upset him.

"Do you have enough evidence to hold him?" My chest felt tight as I said the words. My head was swirling with emotions right now, and I felt certain that if I let my guard down for even a minute, I might pass out.

"Sure I do. Aggravated stalking and resisting arrest, for starters. I'm sure there are other charges we can press also. They'll hold him until we can get a warrant, but I don't foresee that being a problem."

"Good." Leonard needed to be locked up. He had enough crazy in his gaze to leave me unsettled—especially since I seemed to be his focus.

Jackson's eyes latched on to mine. I hesitated, fearing he'd see everything I was feeling. All the fear and confusion and more confusion.

"I know you have to feel shaken," he said.

I didn't bother to deny it. Jackson could read me better than a veteran officer reciting someone's Miranda rights. "I am. I mean, a bounty?"

"That was even more than I expected to hear."

I raised my hand, shielding my eyes from the sun. "Do you think he was telling the truth? Could there be a cop involved in this?"

Jackson's expression darkened. "I have a hard time believing that."

"But why would he lie?"

"I don't know. But until we get to the bottom of this, we need to be extra cautious."

I nodded in agreement, feeling more unsettled by the moment. My mind still raced through everything I'd learned. "Do you think Leonard will offer any more information?"

Jackson didn't say anything for a minute and seemed to contemplate his response. "It's hard to say."

"You don't think he'll offer anything new, do you? He likes flaunting his power over us by remaining silent. And he doesn't like you because he thinks you like me."

Jackson stepped closer and lowered his voice. "I do like you."

I sucked in a quick breath. "Well, at least I've heard one good thing today."

He pulled me toward him, pressing me into his chest. "I'm not going to let him hurt you, Joey."

I believed him. I knew Jackson would do whatever it took to keep me safe. And I loved that about him.

There was just so much other stuff going on though. Realistically speaking, he couldn't be with me all the time.

I just needed to focus on figuring out what was going on. Maybe then, when it was all over, Jackson and I would have an honest chance with each other. Just one more reason to find answers.

I glanced at the rock in my hand. Jackson had given it to me before chasing Leonard. "Do you have the other rocks?" I asked.

"I have pictures."

"Can I see them?" Something had been nagging at the back of my mind—a theory I wanted to test out.

He nodded. "Sure. Why?"

"He said all the answers were there. I want to see these rocks together."

We went to his police sedan, sat inside with the doors locked, and Jackson blared the AC. He found the photos I requested and handed them to me.

I stared at the three rocks together, trying to make sense of them. I turned and twisted the photos until something clicked in place in my head.

My pulse spiked as I stared at the photos. "Look, if I put them together like this, it looks like a symbol, doesn't it? Like these random lines and circles were puzzle pieces that needed to be put together before we could see the whole picture."

As Jackson studied my mishmash of photos and the actual rock, his gaze darkened. "What have you gotten yourself into, Joey?"

"What does that mean?" I didn't like the sound of it.

He outlined something with his fingers, tracing the lines around an image. "Do you recognize that symbol?"

I squinted, hoping something would click. Finally it did. "It's like an upside down U with two lines through it, a circle in the corner, and a line at the bottom. What does that stand for?"

"It's . . ." He let his voice fade with a sigh.

"What is it, Jackson?" He didn't want to say it. Which meant I wanted to hear his conclusion even more.

"It's nothing."

I turned to him, not letting him off the hook that easily. "It's something. What's that symbol mean?"

He pressed his lips together momentarily before finally muttering, "It's one of the symbols for the Barracudas."

The blood drained from my face, and I suddenly understood the gravity of the situation. "What? I thought they disbanded after . . ."

"No, they didn't disband. They regrouped, and they're stronger than ever."

"But . . ." I'd been there when the organized crime henchmen had been taken down. I'd been a part of it. I'd nearly ruined an undercover investigation in the process.

"I know. We only took down one of their arms.

They have people everywhere, and they're becoming more dangerous and more powerful all the time."

"But . . ." Was that all I could say? Apparently.

I felt sure this group had something to do with my dad's disappearance. I just had no way to prove anything.

And now this.

"Here's the thing, Joey." Jackson shifted to face me. "These guys—the Barracudas—aren't going to waste time painting rocks and leaving clues for you."

"No, Leonard left them. He wants me to know something about the Barracudas."

Jackson frowned. "Maybe he wants to lure you into their trap."

I shook my head "Honestly, he doesn't seem like the type to go hardcore like that. He's a loner and too unhinged to be trustworthy in a group like that."

"I agree. But he's trying to tell you something he feels is important."

"What could that be?"

Jackson shifted to face me more. "We've been working a lot of leads around here lately. We've even had to call the state Bureau of Investigation, the FBI, the coast guard—just to name a few. The Barracudas have chosen this area as their hub. Everyone has an eye on them."

"You suspect that they're somehow connected to Morty's death, don't you?" I'd been able to tell that Jackson knew something—something big—that he wasn't allowed to share. Was this it?

"Let's just say that this area has been a hotbed of crime lately. Things that would keep tourists away if they knew."

"The mayor would hate that."

Jackson raised his eyebrows, answering without words.

I kept thinking about the information I'd seen in Billy's place. I wanted to stay quiet about it to avoid conflict and lectures—at least until I knew for sure that what I'd discovered was valuable.

But I knew I couldn't anymore. My conscious was bothering me.

"I have something you need to see," I confessed, dread pooling in my stomach.

"What's that?"

I pulled out my phone and found the photos. "These."

Jackson took the device from me and squinted as he studied the images. "What is this?"

"I'm not sure. But it could be significant to the case." Did I have to say the rest and explain myself? Weren't the photos enough? I already knew the answer, but I was in denial.

Jackson gave me that look of exasperation. "Joey . . ."

I closed my eyes and, before I lost my courage, blurted, "I broke into Billy's house and found it there."

"You did what?" he croaked.

I plucked one eye open. "I broke into Billy's house."

"What in the world were you thinking?"

"I just wanted answers." I really wanted to say that Dizzy made me do it, but I wouldn't throw my friend under the bus. Or had it been my idea? I'd blocked it out.

An image of the movie *Speed* filled my head again. Yep, that was my life.

"You don't break into people's homes to get answers. Especially not Billy Corbina. Do you know what he would have done if he'd caught you?" His voice escalated with frustration.

"Filleted me and fed me to the fish?" I was glad I had thought that through earlier.

"Yes, exactly. Please tell me you'll never do that again, Joey."

I opened my mouth and shut it again. I would love to tell Jackson that, but I also wanted to be truthful. And I knew if push came to shove, I would do whatever was necessary to find the answers.

He raked a hand through his hair. "We'll talk later."

"Okay." It was all I could offer.

He gave me one more look before staring at my phone again. Then his expression broke.

He'd realized something. But what?

"Now it makes sense." He picked up his phone and, before I could ask any questions, called someone. "You need to go pick up Billy Corbina."

My heart spiked. What? But I knew better than to ask too many questions.

He ended the call and turned toward me, his expression even more serious than usual. "I need to get to the station."

I nodded a little too eagerly. "Of course."

"You can come with me."

"I can?" He might as well have said the Academy had decided to give all Oscar nominees an award instead of picking just one in each category. Jackson was actually letting me tag along again.

"Yeah, you might want to hear this," he said.

I wasn't going to argue. "My listening ears are on."

Chapter Twenty-Seven

I TRIED NOT to ask too many questions as we drove, which was easy enough since Jackson was on the phone again. But before we climbed out of the car at the police station, Jackson turned toward me.

"This morning we finally caught one of the people who've been leaving skimmers at local gas stations and ATMs," he said.

Credit card skimmers? That was . . . not what I expected to hear.

"Detective Gardner was handling one of those cases." I hadn't had any clue it might be connected with all this.

"Yes, he has. We've been trying to track down the person bringing the technology to the area—to cut the snake off at the head, so to speak. It may seem like an inconsequential crime, but in reality it can wreak havoc in the victim's life. Cost them money, time, peace of mind. Meanwhile, the criminals behind it rake in the big bucks."

"I didn't realize it was so lucrative."

He nodded. "They get these credit card numbers and then sell them to bidders on something like eBay, only for criminals. The amount these guys make are nearly in competition with what you probably make as an actress."

"And it's all through criminal enterprise."

Jackson nodded. "The worst part is that it's usually only the tip of the iceberg. Kind of like pot is what they call a gateway drug. Well, skimmers are just the start of other crime binges, and it's nearly impossible to catch the guys behind it."

"But you did?" I clarified.

"Apparently Billy has been the one selling the technology to local thugs in the area."

I tried to think it all through. "Is that the business he and Morty went into together?"

"It's quite possible. Those drawings you found appear to be schematics on how to build those skimmers. Those names? Those are probably his buyers."

I straightened. At least something good had come out of my breaking-and-entering binge. "That's great news."

"The information you found helped us put together some other evidence we'd been collecting. Of course, those pictures you took would be thrown out in a court of law for being obtained illegally. But we can get a search warrant for the actual papers. Maybe the information is still there at Billy's place. It could be the lead we've been looking for."

I beamed. I'd helped break a case. Yay for me.

"But you still shouldn't sneak into Billy's house," Jackson said. "Or anyone's house for that matter."

My beam dimmed quickly.

"Does that mean that Billy killed Morty?"

"We don't know."

Another thought hit me. "If Billy did this, then Zane has been falsely accused."

"He's not out of the woods yet," Jackson said, his frown deepening.

"But he's closer to being out of the woods." And that was enough for me.

———

I couldn't believe it, but Jackson let me sit on the other side of the interrogation window as Billy was being questioned. I could hear everything that was being asked and answered.

And I couldn't be happier. Maybe Jackson finally saw me as a vital part of this team. It was doubtful, but a girl could dream.

"I don't know what you're talking about." Billy's arms were crossed, and he was the picture of defiance. He wasn't at all happy about being here or being caught. Then again—who would be?

"The two guys we caught sold you out," Jackson said. He looked all *Law and Order* tough. No, make that Stephen Amell on *Arrow*. I mean, Oliver Queen wasn't officially a detective but close enough. "They said you were the one they got the skimmers from."

Billy scowled. "They just want to frame me."

"Why would they want to frame you?"

"You tell me." The heat in Billy's gaze was capable of burning a hole in anything in its path. "And I didn't kill Morty. I figure that's your next question."

"Then who did?"

"I'd say that's your job to figure out, not mine. Besides, I thought you'd already arrested someone. Zane."

"But we know you and Morty were going into business together. We just didn't know that you were distributing skimmers. Or were you creating them?"

"I don't know what you're talking about."

Another officer went into the room and handed Jackson a paper. He studied it before saying, "You know you hired someone to make them."

Jackson slapped something onto the table.

Probably those schematics.

Billy's gaze darkened. "You went into my house."

"We had a warrant."

He shrugged. "There's nothing illegal about trying to figure out how they're made. Maybe I'm researching for a book or something."

"We all know that's not true. If you didn't make them, who'd you get them from?"

Billy shrugged. "I don't know what you're talking about."

This was better than *Law and Order* or *Arrow*. If only I had some popcorn and an Izze.

"That's not going to cut it, Billy." Jackson leaned closer. "You're going to be in prison for a long time for this. Even your father's money won't buy you out."

His fist hit the table, spilling Jackson's coffee. Jackson made no move to clean it up.

"I don't need my dad's money anymore," Billy said. "I'm making my own."

"Your legal bills will go into the millions. Are you making that much on your own?"

Billy's gaze jerked back up toward Jackson's. "Yes, I am."

"And all from selling these skimmers? Or from your little bar?"

Billy said nothing, but his cheeks reddened. He didn't like Jackson insulting his business.

"Are you a part of the Barracudas?" Jackson pressed.

Billy snorted. "Of course not."

Jackson gave him a cold no-nonsense stare. "We have evidence that says that might not be true."

"The Barracudas have their hands everywhere," Billy said. "Everywhere. You could be working with them and don't even know it."

"It's doubtful."

"I'd tread carefully if I were you." Billy leaned closer. "You can tell your friend Joey that her dad started asking questions like this, and no one has seen him since."

Chapter Twenty-Eight

DETECTIVE GARDNER RUSHED into the room where I was watching the interrogation. He pounded on the glass to get Jackson's attention.

Jackson pushed himself from the table and strode toward the door, his expression stormy at the interruption. He stepped out and shut the door behind him. "What's going on?"

"I knew you'd want to hear this right away," Gardner said. "We've got another dead body."

"Where?"

"A hotel on the oceanfront. We think it's connected to this case."

"You stay here with Billy and see if you can get anything else out of him," Jackson said. "I'm going to the scene."

Gardner nodded and stepped into the interrogation room. As soon as the door was closed, Jackson turned toward me and stooped down until his eyes were even with mine. He did it only when he was really concerned about me. Like now.

"Tell me what you're thinking," he said.

I knew what he was talking about. What Billy had said concerning my dad.

But we didn't have time to address that now. Not really. Instead, I said, "I'm just tired of everyone who has any information about my father refusing to talk."

"We're working on it. We have ways of using leverage, so don't give up hope yet." He straightened, took my arm, and led me to the door. "Come on. Let's get to the hotel."

"I'm coming?" Had I heard correctly?

"Unless you don't want to."

"Oh, I'll go." Of course.

Five minutes later, we were in Jackson's car. I knew I didn't have much time to chat with Jackson, so I jumped right in.

"Billy Corbina is a vile human being," I muttered.

"He is."

"And despite everything we know, we still don't know who killed Morty."

Jackson remained quiet. He was probably still thinking about Zane.

"How about Leonard? Does he know? Is he talking?"

"He's gone stone-cold quiet. Won't say a word."

I sighed. "Gardner said this dead body might be connected also? Can you tell me anything before we get there?"

"It's a woman. Housekeeping came to do their daily cleanup and found her. That's all I know at this point."

I nodded, satisfied that he'd said that much. "Okay, got it."

We pulled up to a hotel a few minutes later. It was

one of the nicer ones in the area with an indoor pool and updated exterior. We took the elevator up to the fifth floor, and I stayed on Jackson's heels as he hurried down the hallway.

"Any idea who she is?" Jackson asked the officer at the scene.

"The front desk said her name was Sydney Becker. I did a quick check, and that appears to be an alias. Couldn't find a driver's license or credit card information even."

"Stay here," Jackson told me.

I nodded obediently and took my place against the wall. All the rooms here were oceanfront, and a wall of windows on the other side of the hallway faced the parking lot and street outside.

Police tape was pulled across the door, and an officer stood guarding the area.

I'd thought I wanted to come, but now I remembered again just how boring this part of police investigations was. I studied my cuticles. Texted Phoebe. Took some silly selfies and played with filters that made me look like a cat and a troll.

Finally, I peeked past the officer and into the room. I spotted the body. With a tattoo. Dark hair. Pierced nose.

I swallowed the lump in my throat just as Jackson spotted me and paced closer to the police line.

"Would the fact that she's Australian make any difference?" I asked.

Jackson paused and stared at me with a touch of trepidation in his gaze. "Why do you think that?"

My anxiety climbed higher. "I've seen her before."

He crossed to the other side of the police line and looked at me. "Where?"

I swallowed hard again. "Billy's place."

"You saw *this* woman there?" He looked dumbfounded. Truly dumbfounded.

One of my many talents was making him feel that way.

"That's correct," I said. "She had an accent. As did the woman who met with Evan and Morty before his death."

He shook his head, obviously exasperated with me.

I shrugged. "You told me to stay out of it."

"Yet you didn't."

"I didn't want you to know that!"

He did the familiar rake-his-hand-over-his-face move. "That doesn't mean that you withhold information."

"I didn't want you to be mad."

"I'm not mad. But your actions concern me sometimes."

I shrugged again. Frowned. Widened my eyes with apology. "Sorry."

He took my elbow and led me to the other side of the police line, toward the body. He lowered his voice as he leaned closer. "Anything else I should know?"

I shook my head, honestly trying to think of something. Anything. "Nothing comes to mind."

As soon as I said the words, something across the room caught my eye.

"She and Billy were apparently more than just colleagues," I said.

"Why would you say that?"

"Because Eau de Sunset was at Billy's place also. She'd stayed there."

He nodded slowly. "Good observation."

An officer—his name was Byron, if I remembered correctly—approached Jackson. "We found her phone and were able to unlock it."

"Anything noteworthy on it?"

The officer showed him the screen. "How about this?"

I glanced over Jackson's shoulder and sucked in a breath.

"That's my mom," I whispered.

———

My whole world felt like it was spinning, and I might have sunk to the floor if it weren't for Jackson grabbing my arm and leading me into the hallway.

"Take a deep breath," he said.

I listened. Sucked in air. Released it. Over and over.

That was my mom. Definitely.

I'd thought I'd seen her about a month ago around the time of my movie premiere here in this area. Then I'd rationalized that my eyes were just playing tricks.

She'd walked out of my life and my father's life when I was two. Said she was going to pursue a modeling career. We'd never seen or heard from her since then. Once—just once—when I was a teenager, I'd tried to find her.

My search had lasted about a week, until I realized she must not want to be found. And she obviously hadn't made a name for herself as a model, because I'd never seen any pictures of her.

When I'd shown up here in the Outer Banks, I'd found some of my father's old things. Tucked among them was a photo of my mom. Not an old picture. A new one. Taken on the grassy shores of what appeared to be a local waterway.

So my dad had seen my mom—or somehow he'd gotten that picture. And not long after that, he'd also disappeared. And now this.

What was going on here?

"Joey?" Jackson peered at me.

I raised a hand. "I'm okay," I insisted.

I had no idea if I was okay or not.

Because if Billy was connected with the Barracudas, and Sydney was connected with Billy, and my mom was connected with Sydney, did that mean my mom was connected with the Barracudas? My stomach squeezed, and I thought I might throw up.

"We don't know what this means," Jackson said.

"You and I both know that this can't be a coincidence." My voice held an unusual edge. I needed Jackson to know that he couldn't just brush this off.

"I'd love to talk to you about this later."

Later? I remembered everything else going on. The dead body. Leonard arrested. Billy arrested.

This was going to be a very busy night for Jackson.

I nodded. "Yeah, later."

Jackson stared at me, apology staining his gaze. "I want to stay with you. To talk to you. I know you need me right now. But I can't walk away from this case."

"I know."

He looked at me like there was more he needed to say, for me to understand. He was worried I couldn't handle this aspect of his life—like Crista might since she grew up around it.

Should he be worried? Could I handle this?

I'd like to say yes. But police work was all consuming.

As was acting. Could our lives work in sync with each other's?

"I want to meet you for breakfast tomorrow, okay? But until then, I need to take you home. There's nothing else for you to see here tonight. And I can't imagine what other movies you're going to act out while you wait."

That got a little smile from me. "Okay."

He reached for the hair at my neck as he leaned toward me, his forehead pressing against mine. "I'm sorry, Joey."

"You have a job to do. Don't apologize. I don't expect you to stop everything for me."

He kissed my forehead. And I realized there was nothing else to say.

Chapter Twenty-Nine

JACKSON DROPPED me back at my place. He checked it out first, deemed everything safe, and then asked me if I'd be so kind as to not leave or go anywhere without him.

I agreed, of course.

Until I remembered that I'd left my favorite lip balm in my car. I figured it couldn't hurt to sneak downstairs quickly and grab it. And it hadn't.

My Berry Blossom Bliss was now in hand, and I hadn't run into any trouble. And my lips were thanking me.

Until I reached the stairwell.

And then I wouldn't really say it was trouble. Winston Corbina was standing there. I remembered my conversation with Leonard, and a startling thought hit me.

Was Winston behind my whole super-stalker fan-club thing?

I wasn't sure. But now wasn't the time to let on that I

might know anything. No, it was too secluded. Too late. And Jackson was too far away.

"If it isn't Joey Darling." He squinted and looked at my face. "That's a nasty knot on your forehead."

"I know. Unfortunate accident." I touched the spot and cringed.

He grimaced. "I'd say."

I stared at him a moment, contemplating my words, before finally saying, "Billy is at the police station."

His eyes narrowed, but I wasn't sure if he was surprised or another emotion. "Is that right?"

"They're saying he killed Morty Savage." I swatted a mosquito. There was usually a nice breeze that kept the skeeters away, but not tonight. Everything was still around me.

Winston snorted. "My son is many things. He's not a killer."

Phoebe's words again echoed in my head, her warning about what drugs did to people. Did Winston have any clue? He was a smart man. I had to think he did. But maybe we were never ready to accept information like that about the people we loved.

"It doesn't matter anyway," Winston continued. "We haven't spoken to each other in weeks."

I nodded and processed that. I wondered what had caused their riff, but with the personalities of these two, the possibilities were endless. "You had a falling out, huh?"

Winston's scowl deepened. "You could say that. But I hope he hasn't gone out and done anything stupid."

"Yeah, me too."

"My son isn't safe to be around, you know." He studied my face.

I drew in a sharp breath, wondering what he was implying. "Is that right?"

"Absolutely. I'd stay far away from him. He hasn't gotten his act together yet."

"I see."

"You're a nice girl, Joey," he said. "I'd hate to see you get mixed up in anything—especially anything that puts your life in danger."

A chill bit me down to the bone. "Me too."

"But I know you have that curiosity. That determination. That sense of justice. Just like your father."

I gripped my lip balm, my throat suddenly tight and achy at the mention of my dad. "You saw that in my father too, huh?"

"It was hard to miss."

I shifted, knowing I shouldn't ask this next question but unable to stop myself. "You know that piece of paper you gave me when we first met?"

His eyes sparkled. "I do."

He'd handed me a note, and I'd foolishly let the wind sweep it out of my hand and into the water. I'd never stopped wondering what he'd written there.

"What did it mean?" I asked, fishing for answers.

"You don't know?"

I licked my lips and shook my head. "No, I don't."

He smiled. "Then I'll have to let you figure it out."

Daggonit! I wondered what the chances were that he might write it again. Slim to none, I'd guess.

"Have a lovely evening, Joey."

I walked inside my condo after we said goodbye. But something drew me back to the window.

I peered out, and I could see the parking lot. Someone scrambled out of a car there. Climbed the stairs to the third story. I could hear the footsteps echoing above me. Hear a door open.

I'd recognized the woman.

It was Crista.

And I knew where her footsteps had led.

To Winston Corbina's.

I moved to my balcony overlooking the Albemarle Sound. I had a lot to think about.

Starting with everything Leonard had said.

To say that conversation had shaken me to the core would be an understatement. Whatever was going on with that little fan club had thrown my world off balance.

Someone was actually funding these people? Paying them for information? Why would they do that?

It had started because they'd all loved *Relentless* and wanted to see it stay alive. How had it morphed into this?

And was Leonard telling the truth about the other members? That he couldn't identify them, but he knew one was a cop, one was a reporter, and one was a friend?

A shiver raked down my spine.

I didn't like the sound of that.

I knew one thing for sure. I wasn't going to extinguish this super-stalker fan club with one swoop. No, there were too many of them. They had too much incentive. And I was in deep trouble.

My thoughts idled over to Billy and then to the dead Australian woman.

So many pieces were falling into place. Yet the main

piece was missing. Who had killed Morty? If no one confessed to it, then how would we ever figure this out?

There had to be a way.

And until I figured that out, I was going to watch *Celebrity Truth or Dare*.

My episode was on tonight.

Chapter Thirty

MY PHONE RANG the next morning as I was getting ready for Jackson to pick me up. I held my breath as an electronic voice asked me to accept a call from Zane Oakley. I said yes and waited to hear his voice on the other line.

"Joey?"

"Zane!" Guilt pounded at me. I should have gone to visit him again. "How are you?"

He didn't answer. "What's going on with the case, Joey?"

I thought about everything I'd learned and then considered what I might be allowed to say—or not say. "We've got some good leads, but we still don't know who framed you."

"Was it Billy?"

I froze in front of the bathroom mirror where I'd been applying my mascara and wondered where Zane had gotten that information. "Why would you ask that?"

"He was brought in here last night. I saw him from a distance."

"He's a suspect. He's definitely been involved in some unscrupulous stuff." I thought about those skimmers and Zane's impromptu trip to South Carolina. "You weren't involved in his newest business venture, were you?"

"No! How could you think that?"

"I had to ask. You haven't been acting like yourself lately." I put my makeup away and did one last check in the mirror. For a girl with a unicorn knot and polka dots, this was going to have to do.

"I was framed for this, Joey. You're right—I haven't made great choices, but I haven't done anything as dumb as getting involved with Billy's businesses."

I really hoped that was true.

"Zane, you said you saw a murder while you were out of town and were running for your life," I started. "And whoever these guys were, they said you had something they wanted."

"Right."

I was about to say, "Tell me more about that," when the truth hit me.

That hadn't happened to Zane. "You took that from an episode of *Relentless*."

The words sounded surreal as they left my lips. How could he do that to me? And then ask for help? He had a lot of nerve.

I waited for him to explain himself.

He was silent for a minute. "You're right," he finally said. "That was a lie. I was trying to think of an excuse to justify my behavior, and that episode came to mind."

My stomach dropped. I hated lies because if a person lied about one thing, they'd lie about anything. Had I mentioned that yet?

"Why would you lie to me about why you came back?" I abandoned the bathroom and grabbed my purse. As I did, I saw I still had five minutes until Jackson arrived. I sat on the couch, needing to find my balance and maybe strangle a pillow in the process.

"I didn't want you to be mad at me for coming back to this area and not telling you."

"Why would I be mad?" Okay, I had been a little mad. But I was even more mad because he'd lied.

His voice dropped, and I could tell this conversation was hard for him. "You know I like you, Joey. I like you a lot. I don't want you to see me like this."

My heart thudded in my ears. Because at one time I thought maybe Zane and I did have a chance with each other. But it was becoming increasingly clear that we didn't. Besides, Jackson was already taking up residence in my heart, way more quickly than I thought possible.

I had to say something. "Zane—"

"Don't respond," he said, his voice pleading. "Please. Not right now. I know how it all sounds. And I know you and Jackson like each other. I didn't want to face it. Not really."

I shut my mouth, but my spirit still felt burdened and heavy. I'd handled plenty of situations incorrectly, so I tried to give grace. But giving grace didn't mean I'd easily trust him again.

"Just know that I didn't do this," Zane continued. "Tell me you believe that. Please."

The operator came on, reminding us that our time was almost up. Whatever I was going to tell him, I had to do it quickly.

"I believe you, Zane. We'll talk about this more when you're released." I sighed. "In the meantime, is there anything else you've been able to think of that might help?"

"There's one other thing," he said. "I keep thinking about it, and I think Abe set me up."

"Why would he set you up? Was he working for Billy?"

Zane snorted. "Billy? No, the two of them can't stand each other."

They couldn't? Did that mean there were two different criminal organizations at play here?

This whole thing was becoming more twisted by the moment.

———

Jackson picked me up a few minutes later, and we went to Oh Buoy, one of my favorite smoothie bars. We only chitchatted on the ride there. It wasn't until after we were at a corner table with Mirlo Sunrises in hand that I spoke what was really on my heart—and it wasn't about Zane.

"Any updates on my mom?" My throat ached as I asked the question.

I watched Jackson's face for any sign of what he was about to say—any signal that he was going to deliver bad news. Compassion softened his gaze and sent my nerves into a frenzy.

"We tried to call a contact on Sydney's phone that we thought was your mom, but the number was disconnected," he said.

My frenzied nerves fizzled with disappointment. The strains of "I Get Around" blared overhead, irritating my already scrambled thoughts. I needed a movie soundtrack that better fit the situation, something like Chopin's *Sonata No. 2* or something.

"Has she turned up on any most-wanted lists?" Words I never thought I'd ask about my mom.

He frowned and kept his voice even as he said, "No, Joey."

"But she's connected with all this . . . this . . . craziness. Crime. Murder." Bile burned my throat as I spoke my thoughts aloud.

Jackson leaned toward me. "Here's what we know. Billy found someone on the dark web who was selling credit card skimmers. He became this guy's point person for the area, and Morty became Billy's right-hand man."

"Okay."

"After the two of them did it for a while, they figured they could branch out on their own and keep even more of the profits. They even got this girl—Sydney—to help them."

"So who exactly was Sydney?"

"She was this Currie guy's assistant. As far as we know, she was the only one who'd ever really seen him. From what Billy told me, this guy was very careful to keep his identity concealed, in case anything ever went down."

"I see." I supposed if you were a criminal, that would be a wise move.

"From what we've been able to piece together, Billy and Sydney were supposed to meet with some potential clients tomorrow. They were hoping to make a deal of some sort with them to buy these other skimmers, ones Billy had made. Essentially, they were stealing clients from this Currie guy."

Double-crossing a criminal? Never a good idea. "How did Sydney die then?"

"The same way Morty did. With a bullet through her chest."

I flinched at the thought. "And the weapon?"

"It belonged to Billy."

I blinked at that information. This sounded eerily familiar to Morty's death and Zane's presumed involvement in it. "So Billy did it? Did he decide she was a liability?"

"Or someone is doing a really good job setting up local bad boys," Jackson finished.

He considered Zane a local bad boy? I didn't even ask, nor did I have time to argue. It was the least of my concerns at the moment.

"I'm assuming you did the same gun residue test?" I asked.

He nodded. "We did. It came back negative—but Billy is smart enough to cover his tracks. He probably scrubbed himself down."

I leaned back and played with my straw. Traced my fingers down the condensation on my glass. "What does all of this mean?"

"We don't know yet," Jackson said.

This whole case was a black hole that swallowed our questions and didn't allow us any answers, wasn't it?

I cringed, knowing there was one other thing I needed to bring up. I didn't know how Jackson would take it or how my words would be perceived. But I was going to say it anyway because you never knew what information could be significant.

"Crista went to Winston Corbina's last night," I blurted.

Jackson squinted as if he hadn't heard correctly. "What?"

I nodded. "It's true. And I don't know why or if it has to do with anything. But I thought you should know, especially since she apparently has a key to your house."

"What would she have to do with Winston?"

"That's the question I've been asking also. Maybe the fact that she lives beside you is no coincidence."

Chapter Thirty-One

I WENT to the station with Jackson, even though I knew it was going to be a long day if I stayed with him there. Still, I couldn't stand the thought of sitting in my condo alone, ruminating on my questions. Thinking about Leonard's words. How a friend, a cop, and a reporter were in this secret society of sorts. I figured the closer I could be to Jackson right now, the better.

I promised Jackson I would try to stay out of his way.

Try being the key word here.

But he was filling out reports in his office most of the morning. I'd tried to read through some of the scripts Rutherford had sent me, but most of them bored me.

A sweeping romantic saga? No thank you.

A sci-fi with aliens invading earth? Same story, different title.

A motorcycle gang with heart? Nope, not my style.

I continued to read for a while before stretching my legs. I just so happened to be walking down the hall when a conversation drifted from the room like sea-foam on the wind.

"She just got a new text message confirming the location they're supposed to meet," Chief Lawson said. "This person obviously doesn't know that she's dead."

"The problem is that we don't have any officers here who can go undercover and pull off an Australian accent," Jackson said.

I froze, excitement rushing over me as I ducked out of sight, still listening.

"Sending someone in is the only way we're going to be able to figure out who she's working with," the chief said. "We can't take a chance that these people will know they're being duped."

"I'm not sure we can pull it together quickly enough," Jackson said. "It takes time to either master an accent or find an officer who's already trained for this."

I stepped into the room and cleared my throat.

"Good day, mates. I know just the person who speaks with a perfect Australian accent." I said those words, of course, with an Australian accent. And a dramatic flair of my hand, as if I was presenting myself to the world.

Everyone in the room turned to stare at me—everyone being Chief Lawson, Jackson, and Gardner.

For a moment, I felt like the center act at a three-ring circus. I lowered my hands and tried to look a bit less dramatic, just for credibility's sake.

Finally Jackson spoke. "That's the worst idea I've heard in a long time."

"We can't put a civilian out there," Lawson said.

"It doesn't sound like you have much choice." I said it again with my accent. Of course. "I trained for three months to perfect this accent for my role in *Wildflower Summer*. My vocal coach says I'm spot on."

It had been a small indie film I'd done in between filming *Relentless* Seasons 1 and 2. Almost no one had seen it, but the whole production had been a good experience.

Especially when I thought about the payoff now.

"It's about more than having the accent down," Jackson said, disapproval darkening his gaze. "What if these people were to ask questions about life in Australia?"

"Well, I know they have studios Down Under that can do the best CGI technology work in the world." That was *something*, wasn't it?

Jackson crossed his arms, obviously unconvinced. "Even if everything else fell into place, that doesn't change the fact that you're a civilian."

He did not like this idea. Not one bit.

"You let me go undercover as a mermaid," I reminded him.

"That was different."

I raised my chin. "Not really."

He scowled. "You have no idea what's involved with this, Joey."

"If I'm wired and you guys are close by, what difference does it make? You'll keep me safe. And I'm guessing that as soon as these people fess up to wanting illegal goods, you'll swoop in and arrest them, right? Because that's what this is about. You need to catch them red handed."

"She might be onto something," Chief Lawson said.

"What will the mayor think when his favorite citizen dies while working with the police? It would be a PR nightmare." Jackson glanced at me and softened his tone. "Not to mention that it would just be tragic, in general. I don't like the idea. Not at all."

"Well, whoever these guys are, it sounds like you don't have any other good leads," I said. "Let me just remind you that if there's one thing I'm good at, it's acting. I can do this for you. I can pull it off."

Jackson and the chief exchanged a look.

"We need to talk," the chief finally said. "If you'd excuse us, Joey."

"Of course."

Whoever these guys were, they were involved in something bad. Something connected with Zane? Morty? My mom?

I didn't know.

But I sure hoped I had the chance to find out.

Against all odds, Chief Lawson and Jackson had agreed to let me do this. There was a whole set of rules and protocols they'd had to go over with me. And when I said go over, I meant over and over and over.

Jackson had been quiet and tense since the decision had been announced. He didn't like this, and I couldn't blame him.

Two people were already dead, and it was difficult to know exactly what I'd be facing.

I looked in the mirror in the single-person bathroom I'd taken over and shifted uneasily. I could do this. I just needed to pretend I was in a movie.

I *felt* like I was in a movie. I wore a wig, fake tattoos had been painted onto my arms, and a magnetic nose ring graced my nostril. I'd donned an outfit similar to the one I'd seen Sydney wear: khakis and a black shirt.

None of those things mattered as much as selling my accent did. I'd been mentally practicing for the last hour. This was the role of a lifetime, wasn't it?

I jogged in place and wiggled my arms to get the tension out, feeling a bit like a boxer about to go in for the big fight.

Hands came down on my shoulders and squeezed them. I didn't have to turn around to know who it was. Jackson.

"Are you sure you want to do this?" he murmured. "No one would blame you if you backed out."

I nodded. "I'm totally sure. How else are we going to find out anything?"

My mom's picture played in my mind. She was the real reason I was so gung ho about this, wasn't she? I already knew the answer. Yes.

"You're not to make any moves. You just get the information, and you're done."

"I can totally do that."

Jackson turned me around until we were face to face. "Joey, I don't like this."

The look in his eyes was pure concern and . . . love? No, not love. He didn't love me. It was too soon. Right?

Something about the look in his eyes captured me. Drew me in. Made me want to never look away.

But I had a job to do first.

"I'm in my element, Jackson. I have to do this."

"I knew you'd say that." His shoulders slumped. "Say the key words, and we'll extract you."

"Is it hot in here?" Yep, those were my key words. I

just hoped I remembered them, and I didn't freeze up like I did with the whole tennis bracelet debacle.

"It's time to go." Detective Gardner tapped at the door.

"Be right there," Jackson said. Before we stepped away, he pulled me into a hug. A long hug. A hug that really said more than any words ever could. I was taking up residence in Jackson's heart also, wasn't I? The thought thrilled me.

Jackson stepped back and looked away—as if looking into my eyes would make him forget his resolve or something. Instead, he took my arm, and we walked outside together. I climbed into the rental the police department had secured for me. Sydney's rental.

With a somber nod at Jackson, I took off. I didn't want to be late.

I drove to the address I'd been given, climbed out, straightened my outfit, and finally walked toward the door. Some evidence had been obtained from the Australian woman's hotel room, and it was now in a briefcase I held.

The good news was that a team of police officers had surrounded the house and were on guard to help at a moment's notice.

Including Jackson.

I'd also been wired, so officers were listening to my every word.

The house was large and oceanfront. Dunes surrounded it on either side, and the front door had been painted a peachy beach color that made the whole place look friendly and unassuming. I swallowed hard before ringing the doorbell.

It's show time.

A moment later, a man I'd never seen before answered. He was of medium height with ruddy skin and buzzed blond hair.

"Sydney, come on in." He glanced behind me, as if making sure I wasn't followed. He must have felt certain because he shut the door.

Panic tried to kick in. I was totally on my own. Maybe this hadn't been a great idea. But I couldn't turn back now.

He led me into the living room, where another man waited. This man was tall with dark hair. Both had a rough edge to them—more of a Billy vibe. They were guys who knew how to handle themselves on the street. Despite that, they still dressed like locals with their cargo shorts and boat shoes. I suspected that was part of their cover—to blend in.

The second man stared at me. "You look familiar."

Tension pinched my muscles. I really hoped he wasn't a *Relentless* fan. "I have one of those faces."

He stared at me another moment, and it took everything in me not to cringe.

"So do you want to talk about my face or the real reason I'm here?" I muttered, trying to maintain an air of cool.

Finally, after another moment of thought, he nodded. "Do you have the goods?"

He was obviously the leader of the two.

I swallowed the lump in my throat and remembered I was acting. If I showed any nerves, it would be a dead giveaway. "Of course. Do you have the cash?"

Dark-Haired's eyes narrowed. "I want to see the goods first."

"As you wish." I opened the briefcase and showed him the skimmers he'd ordered.

I hoped that was what these were, at least. We were winging it here.

"These aren't the ones I wanted," he muttered, picking one up. "Currie promised me the nicer ones that are harder to spot."

My pulse spiked. This wasn't something we'd rehearsed. But I could handle this. I had no choice.

"You'll have to take that up with him." I was certain to keep my voice even.

"It's a little hard to do since we never meet with him."

Good to know. No one had seen Currie—a brilliant move on his part.

"I'll relay the message," I said.

Dark-Haired leered at me. "That's right—you're just a little courier, aren't you?"

"A little courier. You can call me that if you'd like." I figured the best course of action was to be compliant and not make any waves.

"I feel like there's something you're not telling us." The man stared at me with a gleam of malice in his gaze.

"Why would you say that?" I scooted backward, trying not to show my nerves.

"Tell us how to find Currie."

"I don't know how to find him." I wished I did. That would solve so many of my problems.

He glared at me, stepping closer. "I don't believe you."

This was when I needed to hit that panic button. The man's body language screamed danger, from his fisted hands to his growling voice. What was my panic phrase again? My mind went blank.

Tennis bracelet, tennis bracelet, tennis bracelet. It was all I could think about.

"I can think of a way to draw him out." A sardonic look stained Dark-Haired's gaze as he continued to watch me, his gaze traveling up and down my length.

His eyes clearly told me that the way involved me, and I didn't like that thought.

I swallowed hard, trying to think quickly.

Which was something I was never good at.

Finally, I said the only thing that came to mind. "I bet your feet smell really bad when you take those shoes off. Loafers without socks? It's a nightmare."

"What?" Dark-Haired's bottom lip dropped.

They glanced down at their feet. As they did, I took off in a run toward the door. I reached it before they did and flung it open.

When I stepped onto the porch, Jackson grabbed me and pulled me away from the scene.

Police officers rushed in.

And my job was done. A rush of adrenaline and elation swept through me.

"That was a fair dinkum thrill," I said.

"A what?"

"It's Australian for genuine, matey. Now, what do you say we go have a Barbie?"

Jackson's face cracked into a grin. "Let's just get you out of here instead."

Chapter Thirty-Two

"YOU DID A GOOD JOB, JOEY," Jackson told me later when he finally had a moment to step away from the investigation.

I was hanging out in the lounge at the police station, an area where the officers reheated their meals or grabbed a cup of coffee. There was also a sofa, one that seemed especially comforting right now, despite the fact that it smelled like stale coffee.

The sun had set, leaving darkness in its wake. It had been a long day. I'd been able to wash off my tattoos, and I hadn't accidentally inhaled my metallic nose ring. Two for the win. The station was buzzing from everything that had happened though. They were seeing more action in the past few days than they usually saw in a month.

"Thank you." I leaned back on the couch, my fingers wrapped around a mug of coffee, and reviewed everything I knew. "So there's someone—he goes by Currie—who's heading up this arm of an international crime ring. He's selling credit card skimmers to criminals on the East Coast. Billy was one of his main contacts in the area. Billy then took the skimmers and sold them to other low-life criminals in the area."

"That sounds correct."

"But then Billy thought he'd be smart and find someone to make these skimmers for him. He'd eliminate this Currie guy and then get to keep more of the profit. He even talked Sydney, who worked for Currie, into coming over to his side. They were romantically involved with each other."

"You're becoming more like Raven every day."

"The problem is we don't know who killed Morty or who this Currie guy is or how Zane's gun got into the hands of the killer—"

"Unless he *was* the killer. There's a possibility he was helping Billy."

"Did Billy say that?"

He shook his head. "No, he didn't."

"Then there's also the matter of how that package got into Zane's room."

"There's one logical explanation."

I ignored him because I knew exactly what he was getting at: that Zane was guilty. I still wasn't ready for that to be a reality. "Is Abe still behind bars?"

Jackson shook his head. "No, he was released on bond."

"He had money for bond? I wonder how he got that?" I took another sip of coffee as I thought it through.

Jackson stood and grabbed a granola bar from the cabinet. He tossed it to me before grabbing one for himself.

As soon as I felt the crinkly paper in my hands, I

realized I was hungry. But I wasn't finished with this conversation either. "How do we find this Currie guy?"

"We?" Jackson sat back down and raised his eyebrows.

Great, I sounded like Dizzy. "How are *you* going to find him?"

"I don't know."

As I took a bite of my "dinner," my thoughts continued to turn over everything we knew. "Did you talk to that neighbor who saw Morty and Zane talking?"

"Not since that day at the crime scene. Why?"

"I wonder if anything else has come to mind. Or maybe his wife saw something. When I looked up at the house, I saw her just standing there and watching. Did you ever talk to her?"

"No, we didn't," Jackson said. "It's somewhere to start."

A few minutes later, Jackson found the man's information and gave him a call. The name he'd given Jackson at the crime scene was Matt Stephenson, from Baltimore, Maryland.

The call didn't go through though—an electronic voice said the number was no longer in service. Had Jackson written it down incorrectly?

That didn't seem like Jackson.

"Let's visit the realty company and see what number they have," Jackson said. "Because talking to Matt again suddenly seems like a very good idea."

"We're looking for information on the family who was staying here last week," Jackson told a curly hair blonde at the front desk of Corbina Real Estate—yes, it was one of Winston's many enterprises. "Could you help us?"

"Do you have a warrant?"

"No, but the number the man gave us isn't working, and it's of the utmost importance that we talk to them."

She stared another moment before finally nodding. "I suppose I can help, especially since he already gave you his information. What's his name?"

Jackson looked at his paper. "Matt Stephenson."

She typed something into her computer and let out a grunt. "I'm sorry. There's no Matt Stephenson listed in our database."

Jackson looked at the paper where he'd written down the man's information—straight from his driver's license. "That's the name he gave me."

She shrugged. "I don't know what to say. What address was he staying at?"

Jackson rattled it off.

She typed in something else and let out another soft grunt. "No, I'm sorry. There were six college girlfriends staying at that address last week for a reunion."

Jackson and I exchanged a look.

We both knew the truth.

We needed to find Matt Stephenson. Or, should I say, Currie, the King of Fiends.

"Where now?" I asked when we stepped outside.

"There's only one place I can think of: Blackbeard's Pleasure."

We went back to the restaurant, found the busboy, and showed him a picture of Kevin James. Or Matt Stephenson. Or Currie. Whatever his real name was.

And the busboy recognized him as the guy who'd met with Morty last week.

Jackson and I didn't speak until we reached his car.

My thoughts continued to process everything.

Now we knew—most likely—who Currie was but not his real name or where he was currently located. Also most likely, he'd killed Morty. Why else would he go through all this trouble?

He fit the profile.

"I need to get back to the police station and see if I can figure out who this guy really is," Jackson said. "He's obviously using an alias and even gave me a fake driver's license."

"Okay. And I should . . ." I hated the thought of going back to my place.

"I prefer that you stay close. Especially until we know where this guy is. Would you mind coming back to the police station with me?"

"Not at all." In fact, I was hoping he would ask me.

Because I had a feeling this guy—Currie—was a member of the Barracudas. And I had another feeling that the Barracudas had something to do with my father's disappearance.

With every answer I found out about them, I was another step closer to finding my dad.

"Any Leonard updates?" I asked as Jackson started down the road.

"He's gone totally silent," he said. "He won't say a word."

"It's almost like he's enjoying this."

"You and I both know that something isn't right with him."

"No, it's not." I frowned. "I just wished he would give up something, you know?"

Jackson reached over and squeezed my hand. "I know. Just give it time."

We pulled up to the station.

I really, really hoped Jackson could find some answers.

———

As Jackson was doing another round of interrogations with the two men who'd tried to buy skimmers, my thoughts constantly turned like the ocean's tide as I tried to make sense of things. It was no use.

When my phone buzzed with an incoming message, I welcomed the distraction.

I glanced at the screen. Another #JoeyRocks clue?

What? But Leonard was locked up. Had another member of my supposed fan club left it?

I read the numbers there: *503.*

Unlike the earlier clues, those numbers told me exactly where this rock was.

Outside the police station.

I glanced back at the interrogation room where I knew Jackson was. I wouldn't interrupt him.

No, I'd grab the rock and bring it back here for Jackson to see when he was done.

With a touch of hesitation, I headed down the hall, said a few words to the receptionist, and skirted past another officer bringing in a disorderly drunk.

Finally I stepped outside. A gust of wind greeted me, sending my hair in a wild whirlwind motion around my head.

I looked at the picture on my phone again. If I had to guess, the rock was around the corner and not here near the front of the building. I should be okay out here because I was in plain sight, where anyone could see me.

Except no one was around.

That just meant I needed to move more quickly.

As soon as I stepped out of sight, I felt something pressing into my back. Not a gun. A knife.

This had been a setup, hadn't it?

"You don't have to do this," I said, trying to buy time. I straightened—though barely. One wrong move and that knife would cut through my skin.

I glanced around. No one else was back here right now. But cops came and went from this area constantly. If I could only buy myself some time.

"I know what you're trying to do. Get in or you'll regret it."

Well, those options didn't sound great.

But I also knew I wasn't supposed to go anywhere with anyone, that it decreased my chances for survival.

I couldn't even see the man's face, but I somehow knew it was Currie. I recognized his voice.

He'd found me. Here at the police station.

"This is a risky move," I muttered, still standing there as stiff as a board.

"So was the stunt you pulled earlier when you impersonated Sydney."

So he knew about that. Interesting.

"Besides, I'm a risky kind of guy. Let's go."

Sweat trickled down my back. "I'd rather not."

"I'm not playing games."

"I'd say you are. You did leave a rock out here for me to find." *Shut up, Joey. Shut up.*

Apparently talking was my norm when I thought my

life was on the line. That wasn't necessarily a good thing.

"Listen, I'm not going to hurt you. I just want to talk."

Like I'd never heard that line before. "Then why do you have a knife?"

He sighed. "Listen, your mom sent me. She wants to talk to you. I'd rather do this the easy way."

Chapter Thirty-Three

NAUSEA CHURNED in my gut as I rode with the man down the road.

My mind told me this was a really bad idea, but my curiosity propelled me on.

My mom.

Would I finally have answers about her? Why she'd left? What she'd been doing?

I had no idea. And I knew this was probably a mistake.

Yet here I was, and there was no going back.

"Where are we going?" I asked, staring at life around me. Tourists with no clue what was going on. Motorists anxious to grab food or get to the beach. Bicyclists trying to get to work on time.

No one noticed us in this older-model sedan. That was probably the idea. A fancy car would have drawn attention. But this vehicle had seen some years.

"You'll see."

I glanced at Currie—at his soft jaw, his hard eyes.

The lack of anxiety in him right now as he executed whatever plan this was.

He was trained, I realized. A professional. And that thought didn't bring me comfort.

"Do you know my mom?" I asked.

"Maybe."

That wasn't enough for me. I didn't want a one-line pitch. I wanted the whole story. "What's she like?"

"You ask too many questions."

We crossed the causeway that led to Roanoke Island. "You never were staying at that house on the beach. And you finding me at the crime scene wasn't an accident, was it?"

There was a lot more going on here than I realized.

"I was just following orders."

"You've been selling credit card skimmers." He was listening, so I might as well think aloud.

He grunted. "Maybe."

"Isn't there anything more productive you could do with your time? Find cures for diseases. Build houses for the poor. Bathe and feed stray dogs."

"You need to be quiet," he warned.

"I'm just trying to figure out what happened." I leaned back, feeling strangely nonthreatened at the moment. "Billy was working for you as a distributor. He decided to strike out on his own. Meanwhile, I'm guessing that Morty wanted out. In fact, he had evidence against you. I'm also guessing that you stole that when you killed him."

Currie said nothing.

"Maybe it was some skimmers with your fingerprint. Your cell number. A picture of you? I'm going to guess that when you met Morty at Blackbeard's Pleasure, he didn't know who he was meeting. Maybe you lured him there under the guise of another exciting job opportunity. Was that it? Except he realized later that it was you, and that's when he got scared."

Still nothing from Currie.

"Meanwhile, Abe is involved. You got him to take Zane's gun. You knew a scapegoat when you saw one. So you framed Zane. And it worked out perfectly because he'd just bought that gun, he'd snuck back into the area, and he'd been at the gun range earlier in the day. I'm not sure how you knew the two of them were going to meet, but I will say that everything fell into place perfectly for you."

And yet he *still* remained silent. So I kept talking.

"You also realized that Sydney was starting to work for Billy, and you couldn't have that. She knew too much. You needed a way to frame Billy, so you stole his gun. You murdered Sydney, and you were pretty much home free after that, weren't you? Yet you're still here. I would have thought you'd be gone from this area."

Why wasn't he gone? It didn't quite make sense.

"We're wrapping up loose ends," he muttered.

"I see." Was I a loose end?

Before I could blather any more, he pulled to a stop in front of a marshy area in the middle of nowhere—and by nowhere I meant the village of Wanchese. It was a fishing community, but part of it was uninhabitable.

Like where we were now.

"Get out," he grumbled. "And don't do anything stupid."

My hands trembled as I climbed from the vehicle, and the gravity of the situation hit me.

Would my mom really be here? Or was this just an

elaborate setup so someone else could take me out? If that was the case, then I'd fallen for it hook, line, and sinker.

He started down a sandy path, and I decided to follow. I scrambled to keep up. Bugs nosedived at us, but I didn't even care. My need for answers outweighed my discomfort.

Finally, we reached the sandy banks. Gentle waves from the Roanoke Sound lapped at our feet, and crabs darted away from us to the safety of the grasses stretching into the water

Then I waited. Anticipated. Worried.

This could either pay off big time, or I could leave here in a body bag. I knew what my vote was for.

A boat appeared in the distance, and my pulse spiked. I watched as it drew closer and closer and closer.

Two people were on board. A man was behind the wheel, and a woman wearing sunglasses and a ball cap stood behind him.

The boat puttered closer and closer to the shore. I held my breath, watching as the woman hopped out the back and sloshed through ankle-deep water. Finally, she reached me.

I sucked in a breath as her features came into focus.

She looked a lot like me, except she was taller. We were both slender with long dark hair and classic features. But there was a hardness to her that I didn't recognize. She wasn't a nurturing mother figure. She looked like a cold-blooded killer.

When she slipped off her glasses, all the air left my lungs.

This really was my mom. Something in my gut seemed to confirm it.

How did I even greet the woman who'd abandoned me? Emotions collided inside.

She observed me a minute, and her eyes softened. "Josephine. You are one beautiful woman. I always imagined what you'd be like one day when you grew up, and you have far exceeded all my expectations."

"You didn't stick around long enough to find out what I'd be like," I said, a bitter edge creeping into my voice.

Her eyebrows flounced upward. "I deserved that. I have many, many regrets in my life. You're one of them."

My mouth dropped open. "Me being born is one of your regrets?"

"No, dear. Leaving you behind."

My irritation returned, stronger than ever. "That was your choice."

"It was complicated." She flinched ever so slightly, and her expression morphed into a scowl.

"I guess modeling didn't take off?"

The scowl deepened. "No, it didn't work out as I planned. I got in the wrong crowd, some might say. And now here I am."

"You're a Barracuda." It disgusted me to think that someone who'd given birth to me would ever succumb to this.

"You've been doing your homework." She almost sounded impressed.

My hands balled into fists so tightly that my nails cut into my skin. "How could you work with people who are responsible for horrible things?"

"We're not horrible," she said. "We're working for a greater good."

"A greater good? What kind of greater good?"

"I can't tell you that. We aren't even supposed to be talking. The only reason we're meeting is because you won't back off, and I'm here to ask you to do so."

"Oh, my estranged mom, who I haven't seen in more than twenty years, wants me to help her out. Of course I will." My sarcasm bit deep, and I didn't even care. "You've done so much for me."

"Joey." Her voice softened. "I know how this must seem, but I really am trying to look out for you."

"You could have looked out for me by giving me advice on men or wearing bad makeup or how to avoid zits. All this advice is coming a little late."

She stepped closer. "I'll never be able to make up for what I did. For leaving you and your dad. But I can't see you get hurt, Joey. Resent me all you want, but I'm the only reason you're alive right now."

I shivered at her words.

Chapter Thirty-Four

I FINALLY FOUND MY VOICE. "Is that right?"

It was the best reply I could come up with.

"We can't let anything get in the way of our plan, sweetheart. And you're always right there in the middle of things. You're too pretty to die. You have too much of life ahead of you. You should go back to Hollywood and forget all of this."

That made me want to stay here even more.

Another thought struck me, sending a surge of hope through my veins. "Do you know where Dad is?"

Her gaze darkened, and she stepped back. "I don't."

I knew enough about body language, thanks to my acting coach, to pinpoint deceit. She was definitely lying to me.

"Did you do something to him?" I demanded.

"I didn't."

"Tell me the truth. I need to find Dad." My voice lowered to a growl.

"It's better if he's hidden. He's more likely to stay

alive. The two of you are cut from the same cloth, you know."

That didn't do it for me. I needed to know more. "So you talked to him? He knew you were in this area? Is that what got him into whatever mess he's currently in?"

"We were never supposed to run in to each other." She glanced at her watch and slid her glasses back on. "I need to go. My time is up."

Desperation clawed at me. "I need more answers."

"You need to go back to Hollywood. The consequences are dire, Joey. I don't know how much longer I can protect you."

"But—"

"No. No more." She touched my face, but I flinched. "I've always loved you, and I always will, despite what you might think."

Before I could say anything else, she sloshed back through the water and onto the boat. The driver wasted no time taking off. Going . . . who knows where?

Currie turned toward me. "Let's go."

I'd nearly forgotten he was there, but as I looked at him now, ice-cold fear rushed through my veins.

I was still reeling from my conversation with my mom.

My mom.

She was alive. I still couldn't believe it. Not only that, but she was involved with an international crime ring. And she was most likely a felon.

How had my life turned out like this? It was never supposed to happen this way. In all the scenarios I'd run through where I was reunited with my mom, she'd never been some type of Terminatrix.

I glanced over at Currie as we headed away from the meeting. He didn't seem pleased, but that wasn't unusual. His gaze was set as we started toward the causeway leading back to Nags Head. His fingers gripped the steering wheel before loosening and gripping it again.

He was nervous, I realized.

And that fact made me nervous. I needed to get out of this car. Now.

"How about you let me go here?" I nodded toward the walkway running beside the road. "I'll walk back. I need some exercise anyway."

"I'll drop you off."

"I don't mind walking."

"You're not walking!" he snapped.

I swallowed hard and glanced around the car, trying to think of a way to get out of this.

He wasn't going to drop me off and be on his merry way. I could feel the danger looming on the horizon.

"My mom will never forgive you if you hurt me," I said, rubbing my hands on my jean shorts.

"Your mom doesn't realize what a liability you are. You've seen our faces. You know too much. I have orders from the top to take care of you. The Lux will take care of your mom."

That didn't sound good. And who was the Lux? I'd ponder that later.

Think, Joey. Think. You've got to get out of this somehow.

And as always, I defaulted back to *Relentless*. Had Raven ever been in a situation like this? All those

241

episodes, all five seasons, played in fast-forward through my mind before stopping on 204.

Actually, Raven had been in a similar situation with an ex-FBI agent who'd joined the mob.

I swallowed hard again. The causeway was coming up. That might be the perfect time to enact this plan.

It was now or never, I realized.

In one fluid motion, I hit the button on Currie's seat belt, releasing his restraints. At the same time, I reached over and jammed my foot on the accelerator.

"What are you—" he started.

Before he could finish his statement, I jerked the wheel toward the cement barrier on my right. The car slammed into it.

Currie lurched forward in his seat. His head hit the windshield as the car came to a sudden halt. The vehicle was old enough it didn't have airbags. Thank goodness. I never thought I'd say that, but airbags would have ruined my whole plan.

Horns blared, and cars swerved around us, trying to miss us.

I sucked in a deep breath as I stared at him.

It had worked.

The impact of the crash had knocked him out. Meanwhile, my seat belt had saved my life.

Good job, Joey.

But then I zoomed out on the situation.

I realized we were dangling on the edge of the bridge.

Chapter Thirty-Five

I SUCKED in a breath as the car shifted toward the water.

Honestly, I'd thought we'd crash against the guardrail. I'd never expected to crash through it. My problem was that I hadn't had much time to think.

I could hardly breathe as I contemplated my options.

First, I needed to take my seat belt off.

With trembling hands, I reached down and hit the button.

As I did, the car shifted again.

I sucked in a scream.

One wrong move, and this whole vehicle was going over the edge. My head spun at the realization.

I gripped the armrest beside me and tried to control my breathing, to think clearly.

Okay, first I needed to put down my window. Then maybe I could climb out.

Maybe.

I hit the window button, but then I realized that the

car's computer system had shut down on impact. Nothing was getting any power—including the window.

Why couldn't this be an old-fashioned car with crank windows? That would make my life too easy, wouldn't it?

I glanced at Currie again, at his figure as it hunched over the wheel. Blood trickled from his lip and forehead, but his chest still rose and fell. He was alive but knocked out cold.

He was still unconscious. That was the good news.

Without turning my head, I could sense the crowd around me. They were all watching, waiting to see what would happen. Thankfully, no one had touched the car. If they did . . . I dreaded to think what might happen.

Hopefully someone had called 911, at least.

Okay, think, Joey. What do all those experts tell you to do in a situation like this?

I could open a door.

But as I glanced beside me, I realized the metal was crumpled. This door wouldn't open. At least not without a lot of force. That very force would rock the equilibrium of the car and most likely send it toppling into the water below. The back door on my side was pressed against the cement guardrail, so I doubted it would open either.

I had to think of another way.

I needed to break the glass, I realized.

How did I do it without moving too much, and what tools did I have at my disposal?

I thought back through all the random facts I'd ever tried to memorize. That was when one hit me.

Without moving anything but my arms, I reached behind me. Feeling my way around, I managed to get the headrest off. I stared at the two metal prongs that had locked it into the seat. Theoretically, they should be able to crack the glass.

I hoped.

If this worked, I could thank whichever friend had shared the tip on Facebook. And I could thank Eric for beating me down enough that I didn't want to leave the house, so I'd stared at social media instead.

The car shifted again. The crowd around me gasped. Someone yelled.

My stomach dropped as the vehicle rocked toward the water.

My body shifted forward until all I could see was the turbulent waves beneath me.

This wasn't good.

At that moment, I noticed that police lights flashed somewhere in the distance, mingling with the sad, urgent sound of a siren . . . or two.

Then I heard his voice.

Jackson's. He was . . . beside my car, if I had to guess.

"Joey, we're going to get you out of there," he said. "Just stay calm and don't make any sudden moves."

I nodded, unable to find my voice.

But I knew the truth. I had to break this glass if I even had a chance.

With a deep breath, I shoved the prongs into the rubber seal around the window. Giving it everything I had, I wedged the metal into the space.

A small crack appeared.

I released the air in my lungs. Okay, at least it was semi-working.

And the car didn't shift again. That was a good sign.

"A wrecker is on the way, Joey," Jackson continued.

I wanted to look at him, but I didn't think I could stand to see even a touch of fear or concern in his eyes. I just needed to stay focused.

I had to do this again.

So I did.

The glass cracked a little more this time.

Third time's a charm, right?

I jammed the metal into the window one more time. This time it shattered.

My muscles went limp with relief.

But it was short lived.

The car rocked again. I screamed, using every ounce of my strength not to lurch forward. If I did, my body weight would send the vehicle into the water below. I had no doubt about it.

"Joey . . ." Jackson said.

"My mom is a part of an international crime ring, Jackson," I told him, just in case I didn't make it out of this alive. "This guy, Currie, works for her. There's someone else above her, but I don't know who. They call him the Lux. They claim to be working for the greater good, whatever that means."

"Why don't you tell me this once you're out of the car?" Jackson said.

"I'm telling you now, just in case I don't make it."

"You're going to make it, Joey."

"Currie killed Morty and Sydney. Abe helped him set up Zane and Billy. Billy is guilty of the whole skimmer scheme, but he didn't kill Sydney."

"We'll have plenty of time to talk about this later, Joey."

I felt woozy all over. The car was rocking, rocking, rocking. One gust of the wind. One wrong move by a spectator. One wrong move by me . . . and I was going over the edge.

"Finish knocking the glass out of the window," Jackson said. "Move slowly, carefully."

His words finally settled in my mind, and I nodded. Using the metal, I brushed the broken shards out of the way until the window was mostly cleared.

"Joey, I'm going to reach for you. I need you to take my hand."

I liked the idea, but the execution was a whole 'nother story. It required moving and shifting, two things I wasn't comfortable with. "I don't know if I can do that, Jackson."

"Sure you can," he said. "It's going to be frightening. The car might fall. But I'm not going to let go of you, do you understand?"

The thought sent terror rippling through me.

The car swayed again.

The crowd gasped.

Finally, I nodded, realizing I didn't have much time. "Okay."

"I'm reaching out my hand," Jackson said.

I turned my head. Saw him standing there. Saw his outstretched arm.

All I had to do was grab it.

But I knew when I shifted my weight, the car was going over the edge.

"Take my hand, Joey," Jackson pleaded, his voice calm and in control.

The thought of moving froze me. I didn't want to do it. I didn't want to live this out in my life. No, I wanted to wake up and discover this was all a nightmare.

But I couldn't.

"You can do it," Jackson continued. "That storm is stirring up some winds, Joey. We don't know when the next gust might blow through. We don't have much time."

Be brave. Be like Raven.

I closed my eyes. Drew in a breath.

But before I could move, the car groaned and began falling.

Chapter Thirty-Six

I HELD MY BREATH, but things seemed to move in slow motion beside me.

The car had fallen a good two feet probably, but it was still on the causeway.

"Joey, you need to move," Jackson said. "Now."

He was right. I had to do this. And I had to do it quickly and without hesitation.

Currie groaned beside me, coming to.

That was all the motivation I needed.

I twisted and clutched Jackson's arm with both my hands.

As I did, the car pitched again.

I clung to Jackson with all my might.

He yelled something and let out a grunt.

And then the world fell from around me.

I screamed. Closed my eyes. Heard a terrible noise. I waited for an impact.

But there was none.

Instead, my body launched into the air. I hit some-thing soft. Semi-soft, at least.

I forced my eyes open, clueless about what I'd see. If I'd crossed into the afterlife. If I was delusional and surrounded by a watery grave.

No, I was on top of Jackson. His strong arms encircled me. His plan had worked.

He'd been able to heave me out of the car. The impact had propelled us both back and onto the causeway.

Jackson tightened his embrace as the crowd around us cheered.

"Are you okay?" he murmured.

I went limp with relief and then with delirium at the fact that I'd actually survived. *I'd actually survived!*

But what about Currie? He'd gone down with the car. Could he survive a fall like that? It was doubtful.

I released my breath and remembered Jackson's question. "Yeah, I'm okay. But I really could have used a stunt double back there."

———

The TV in the corner of the police department's break room drew my attention. Jimmy Fallon was on, and he was showing blooper clips from *Family Secrets*, all set to the song "Eternal Flame." It was hilarious.

I hugged my coffee mug and listened as he came on afterward. "I know Joey Darling, and you know what's so great about her? She's relatable. She's real. She even admits to being a klutz."

The clip cut to video reel of my earlier accident. "We just heard a report that a taxi driver who was transporting Joey nearly ran off the bridge. Look at that dramatic footage. We're just glad she's okay."

I glanced at Jackson. "They didn't waste any time."

He shook his head and cut the TV off. "No, there are wannabe reporters everywhere."

I sighed. "Tell me about it."

Jackson heaved in a deep breath and leaned forward, his elbows propped on his knees. "So your mom is a part of Barracuda?"

I nodded.

"And she said they're working for a greater good?"

"That's what she said. I have no idea what it means." I'd been thinking about it ever since my thoughts started to clear.

"And your mom knows about your dad?" Jackson asked.

He'd removed himself from this investigation, citing personal involvement, and this was the first real chance we'd had to talk.

I nodded and took another sip of my coffee. "She doesn't appear to know where my dad is. But he apparently saw her, and that was the start of his trouble. That's my impression, at least."

Jackson wrapped his arm around my shoulder. "I'm sorry, Joey."

I nodded. "Me too."

"But I'm so glad you're okay. You gave me a good scare back there."

"How'd you find me?"

"Officer Sanders saw you leave with someone. He knew something was up. He had a description of the car. I put out an APB and then went through forty-five minutes of anguish trying to find you until someone reported that accident on the causeway."

I squeezed his hand. "I'm sorry."

He squeezed back. "I really don't want you staying alone until we know what's going on. For all we know, there could be a hit out on you."

"You really think so?"

"We don't know. But obviously everyone in the Barracudas doesn't listen to your mom. There's someone else higher up who's calling the shots. You could have died today." His voice caught.

"But I didn't."

"You must have some guardian angel."

I turned toward him. "Maybe that's you."

He closed his eyes and pressed his lips into my hand. I could see the deep-seated emotion in him, the inspiring self-control, and again I could read just how much he cared for me. Seeing that meant the world to me.

"By the way, I talked to Crista the other day," he started, visibly pulling himself from the moment. "I asked her if she knew Winston Corbina."

I swallowed hard. "How did she react?"

"With a little confusion. But I tried to sound casual and just mentioned that you had seen her over there. I told her that I didn't realize the two of them knew each other."

"What did she say?"

"She said she met him at the rock-painting event," Jackson said.

Winston had been there? That seemed suspicious within itself.

"He mentioned he might be interested in making a donation for some school supplies," Jackson said. "They were meeting to talk about some fundraising possibilities."

"At ten at night?"

Jackson shrugged. "That's what she said."

If Winston wanted to donate money, he could easily write a check. He didn't need to meet with an up-and-coming teacher about it. But still, Crista and Winston's relationship was the least of my worries at the moment.

"There's good news also," Jackson said.

"I'm ready for some good news."

He nodded toward the door. As he did, Zane stepped through. All my worries seemed to dissolve with a whoosh of air through my lungs.

"I'll give you two a minute." Jackson stepped from the room.

As soon as he was gone, I crossed the room and threw my arms around Zane, who didn't smell anything like Zane anymore. No, he smelled like stale clothes and generic shampoo. But I didn't care.

"They let me go," Zane said. "Thanks to you."

"I'm glad the truth finally came out," I said, clutching his arms. He'd been a good friend to me, and I'd missed him lately—despite our history. "This guy—Currie—he's the one who killed both Morty Savage and Sydney Becker. Abe helped him set you and Billy up."

"Did they ever find him? Or his body?" Zane dropped onto the couch, still looking unusually melancholy.

"They're still searching."

Zane frowned.

"I know it's strange not knowing what happened to him, if he somehow managed to survive or if the current simply dragged him out to sea."

"I don't know what his fate was. I just know that I don't like any of this."

I squeezed his arm. "The important thing is that you've been released."

"But my reputation has already been tarnished."

"Once people hear that you're innocent, they'll change their tune."

He frowned again. "No one wants a Realtor who's been locked up for murder."

My heart panged with grief for him. "Opinions can change. Believe me. Just give it some time."

He jerked his gaze up to meet mine. "I need a favor, Joey."

Whenever someone said that, all of my muscles wanted to tighten like Scarlet O'Hara's corset. I almost never came out on the winning side of things. "What is it?"

"Could I crash at your place for a while?"

My throat tightened. "At my place?"

"You have three bedrooms, right?"

I nodded. "I do."

"I don't have anywhere to go. I don't want to move in with my friends. I know where that will lead. I just need a little while to get back on my feet."

Even though Jackson and I weren't officially dating, I wondered what he would think of that. He probably wouldn't like it. Although he had mentioned me not staying by myself . . .

How could I throw Zane out there by himself when he needed someone? He was right—if he stayed with his old crowd, it would only lead to trouble.

What kind of friend would I be if I refused to help him?

Yet it seemed so complicated.

"Please, Joey." His eyes pleaded with me. "You know

I wouldn't ask unless I had nowhere else to turn. I promise—I won't do anything inappropriate."

My compassion won out over my good sense. I hoped I didn't regret it. "Okay. You can stay—but only for a month. And we're strictly roommates."

He nodded. "Of course. I know you and Jackson have a thing going on."

"I don't want any of your friends over," I continued.

"Okay."

"And at the first sign of trouble, you'll have to get out. No drugs. No drinking. No partying."

"I can do that."

I swallowed hard. "Okay then."

But even as I said the words, I realized this was a horrible idea.

Chapter Thirty-Seven

FOUR DAYS LATER, I stood on a small little stage at the park down the street, surrounded by rock-painting enthusiasts.

As I waited for my turn, I reviewed everything that had happened over the past week.

Leonard was locked up for stalking and sending threats.

Billy was locked up for buying and distributing skimmers.

Currie's body had never been found.

Mom was long gone.

Zane and I were doing okay with our temporary arrangement.

Jackson had been working really hard on wrapping up his cases.

No decision had been made about my future. I'd managed to talk Rutherford into buying me some time to make a choice on some scripts.

The part about tennis bracelet hadn't been cut from *Celebrity Truth or Dare*—but a jeweler had offered an endorsement deal for a new line of . . . what else? Tennis bracelets.

"And now I'd like to present you with Joey Darling," Annette said.

The crowd clapped. I looked out and saw Jackson standing there, keeping an eye on me. Like always. I sent him a smile. And then I launched into my spiel.

"When Annette told me about this project and her goal for raising all this money, I was immediately intrigued," I said. "I know a good cause when I see it."

I paused and gathered myself as my heart pounded furiously in my ears.

"I'd like to dedicate my money for the We Can Fight Cancer Fund to Claire Sullivan," I said. "I didn't know Claire. I never had the chance to get to know her. But I know her sister, who's a wonderful person, and I've gotta think Claire was like that too—that the two were cut from the same cloth."

My gaze found Jackson. I offered him what I hoped was a kind smile. I really hoped I wasn't overstepping my bounds.

I sucked in a deep breath before continuing.

"And I also know a very special man who loved her," I said. "And if he loved her, then I know she was an extraordinary woman because he is an extraordinary man. So I dedicate this project to Claire Sullivan."

I handed my check to Annette. She hugged me as everyone applauded.

This was all to raise awareness, I reminded myself. Not to put the spotlight on myself. The lines felt so blurry and uncertain at times.

I glanced at Jackson again.

He was still staring at me with an unreadable look in his eyes.

I'd overstepped, I decided. He was a private person. I should have asked him first before I brought up Claire. What if he thought I was trying to get publicity for myself from her death?

Unease grew in my stomach.

Despite that, I stood there for the rest of the ceremony. As soon as it was over, I said a few words to Annette. Then I slipped offstage and walked toward the back to compose myself. Later, I'd need to sign some autographs and mingle.

But for right now, there was only one thing I could think about: How was I going to make this right?

Just then, I felt a hand on my bicep. I turned around and saw Jackson standing there. His gaze reminded me of deep waters. But was the depth full of gratitude? Or were they calm depths with unseen turbulence beneath?

I licked my lips. "Jackson," I started. "Maybe I should have—"

He stepped toward me and lowered his voice. "Can I say something first?"

The lump in my throat grew larger, but I nodded. "Of course."

He rubbed his lips together, his gaze still intense. I knew whatever he was about to say, it wasn't something he was taking lightly. I tried to brace myself. Had this been my biggest blooper yet?

"Joey, when I first met you, I had no idea what to think—except that I needed you to stop interrupting my police investigation. I thought you were a little crazy and really beautiful. But I figured you'd be stuck up and full of yourself and part of the Hollywood elite. I also thought you were fascinating and unlike anyone I'd ever met before."

My heart pounded in my ears as I waited for him to finish.

"But then I got to know you. To know you beyond Joey Darling, the actress. And I discovered someone who was not only fun and beautiful but who deeply cares about other people. Who isn't a spoiled little starlet who insists on having an entourage around her."

"Entourages are so three years ago." I winked, but then turned serious again.

"People love you because you're real, I've realized." He appeared unfazed by my offhandedness. "You constantly think about other people above yourself. You've been through the fire, and you've come out even more beautiful."

His words made me freeze. Made me aware of only Jackson, no one else around us. Made me unable to look away from his gaze.

He reached for me, and his hands cupped my face. "Not many women would do what you did tonight, Joey. It really meant a lot to me that you weren't afraid to talk about Claire."

"I meant every word I said."

His gaze burned into mine. "I know. And Joey, I meant it when I said I wanted to give you time to get over Eric. But I've also realized that I would be a fool to ever let you go."

My heart nearly beat out of my chest as his words settled on me.

I hadn't scared Jackson away yet. And I hoped I never did.

Before he could say anything, I reached up and

pulled his head toward mine. My lips met his, and every-thing around us disappeared. It was just the two of us. And it felt wonderful.

"Joey, can I get your picture?" A camera flashed.

Jackson and I pulled away from each other. My cheeks heated—not with embarrassment but with emotion and exhilaration.

We didn't acknowledge the photographer, though he continued to take pictures. I didn't even care.

As I started to step away, I glanced down at the packet of papers I'd been given for this event. That was when I saw a folded piece of paper there with my name scrawled on it.

Weird.

I stopped for a minute and opened the paper.

There was an address written there: 15187 Sandy Shoals Dr.

I showed Jackson, and our gazes met.

I'd solved another mystery. So now my super-stalker fan club was sending me another clue.

An address? What did this mean? What would I find if I went there?

I had no idea, but I had a feeling it had something to do with my father. I grabbed my keys.

I had to find out. Now.

Also by Christy Barritt:

The Worst Detective Ever:

Ready to Fumble (Book 1)

I'm not really a private detective. I just play one on TV. Joey Darling, better known to the world as Raven Remington, detective extraordinaire, is trying to separate herself from her invincible alter ego. She played the spunky character for five years on the hit TV show *Relentless*, which catapulted her to fame and into the role of Hollywood's sweetheart. When her marriage falls apart, her finances dwindle to nothing, and her father disappears, Joey finds herself on the Outer Banks of North Carolina, trying to piece her life back together away from the limelight. A woman finds Raven—er, Joey—and insists on hiring her fictional counterpart to find a missing boyfriend. When someone begins staging crime scenes to match an episode of Relentless, Joey has no choice but to get involved.

Reign of Error (Book 2)

Sometimes in life, you just want to yell "Take two!" When a

Polar Plunge goes terribly wrong and someone dies in the icy water, former TV detective Joey Darling wants nothing to do with the subsequent investigation. But when her picture is found in the dead man's wallet and witnesses place her as the last person seen speaking with the man, she realizes she's been cast in a role she never wanted: suspect. Joey makes the dramatic mistake of challenging the killer on camera, and now it's a race to find the bad guy before he finds her. Danger abounds and suspects are harder to find than the Lost Colony of Roanoke Island. Will Joey find the killer? Or will her mistake-riddled streak continue?

Safety in Blunders (Book 3)

My name is Joey Darling, and I'm a disgrace to imaginary detectives everywhere. When actress Joey Darling discovers a mermaid tail with drops of fresh blood on it while hiking in a remote nature preserve, she knows something suspicious is going on. As details surface, Joey realizes she's dealing with a problem she has encountered one too many times: someone desperate for fame who falls victim to a predator. With the help of her neighbor Zane Oakley and the opposition of local detective Jackson Sullivan, Joey hunts for answers, unaware of the deadly net in which she's about to entangle herself. Joey knows she's a fish out of water when it comes to cracking cases, but can she use her talent—acting—to help find the missing woman? Or will Joey end up swimming with sharks?

Join the Flub (Book 4)

There's no business like show business . . . especially when a killer is involved. Joey Darling's local movie premiere was supposed to be a win-win for everyone involved. But things go awry when the event is sabotaged and Joey's stunt double is seriously injured. Suspects seem sparser than quality G-rated movies, and police fear the intended target was actually Joey. Detective Jackson Sullivan and neighbor Zane Oakley—two men competing for Joey's affection—insist on trading off guard duty until the bad guy is behind bars. To make matters even worse, Joey's ex shows up right before the release of his tell-all book about his life with the Hollywood sweetheart. Someone seems determined to create real-life drama. But Joey isn't one to be deterred. Though a movie-worthy villain wants to pull the plug on this production—and maybe even on a few people's lives —Joey is determined that the show must go on.

Blooper Freak (Book 5)
Joey's friend is accused of murder and the mysterious fan club stalking Joey has answers she desperately needs. With each new case, the Hollywood starlet edges closer to the truth about her missing father.

Flaw Abiding Citizen (Book 6)
Coming in November

Squeaky Clean Mysteries:

***

Hazardous Duty (Book 1)

On her way to completing a degree in forensic science, Gabby St. Claire drops out of school and starts her own crime-scene cleaning business. When a routine cleaning job uncovers a murder weapon the police over-looked, she realizes that the wrong person is in jail. But the owner of the weapon is a powerful foe . . . and willing to do anything to keep Gabby quiet. With the help of her new neighbor, Riley Thomas, a man whose life and faith fascinate her, Gabby seeks to find the killer before another murder occurs.

Suspicious Minds (Book 2)

In this smart and suspenseful sequel to *Hazardous Duty*, crime-scene cleaner Gabby St. Claire finds herself stuck doing mold remediation to pay the bills. Her first day on the job, she uncovers a surprise in the crawlspace of a dilapidated home: Elvis, dead as a doornail and still wearing his blue-suede shoes. How could she possibly keep her nose out of a case like this?

It Came Upon a Midnight Crime (**Book 2.5**)

Someone is intent on destroying the true meaning of Christmas—at least, destroying anything that hints of it. All around crime-scene cleaner Gabby St. Claire's hometown, anything pointing to Jesus as "the reason for the season" is being sabotaged. The crimes become more twisted as dismembered body parts are found at the vandalisms. Someone is determined to destroy Christmas . . . but Gabby is just as determined to find the Grinch and let peace on earth and goodwill prevail.

Organized Grime (**Book 3**)

Gabby St. Claire knows her best friend, Sierra, isn't guilty of killing three people in what appears to be an eco-terrorist attack. But Sierra has disappeared, her only contact a frantic phone call to Gabby proclaiming she's being hunted. Gabby is determined to prove her friend is innocent and to keep Sierra alive. While trying to track down the real perpetrator, Gabby notices a disturbing trend at the crime scenes she's cleaning, one that ties random crimes together—and points to Sierra as the guilty party. Just what has her friend gotten herself involved in?

Dirty Deeds (**Book 4**)

"Promise me one thing. No snooping. Just for one

week." Gabby St. Claire knows that her fiancé's request is a simple one she should be able to honor. After all, Riley's law school reunion and attorneys' conference at a posh resort is a chance for them to get away from the mysteries Gabby often finds herself involved in as a crime-scene cleaner. Then an old friend of Riley's goes missing. Gabby suspects one of Riley's buddies might be behind the disappearance. When the missing woman's mom asks Gabby for help, how can she say no?

The Scum of All Fears (Book 5)

Gabby St. Claire is back to crime-scene cleaning and needs help after a weekend killing spree fills her work docket. A serial killer her fiancé put behind bars has escaped. His last words to Riley were: *I'll get out, and I'll get even.* Pictures of Gabby are found in the man's prison cell, messages are left for Gabby at crime scenes, someone keeps slipping in and out of her apartment, and her temporary assistant disappears. The search for answers becomes darker when Gabby realizes she's dealing with a criminal who is truly the scum of the earth. He will do anything to make Gabby's and Riley's lives a living nightmare.

To Love, Honor, and Perish (Book 6)

Just when Gabby St. Claire's life is on the right track, the unthinkable happens. Her fiancé, Riley Thomas, is shot and in life-threatening condition only a week before their wedding. Gabby is determined to figure out who pulled the trigger, even if investigating puts her own life at risk. As she digs deeper into the case, she discovers secrets better left alone. Doubts arise in her mind, and the one man with answers lies on death's doorstep. Then an old foe returns and tests everything Gabby is made of —physically, mentally, and spiritually. Will all she's worked for be destroyed?

Mucky Streak (**Book 7**)

Gabby St. Claire feels her life is smeared with the stain of tragedy. She takes a short-term gig as a private investigator—a cold case that's eluded detectives for ten years. The mass murder of a wealthy family seems impossible to solve, but Gabby brings more clues to light. Add to the mix a flirtatious client, travels to an exciting new city, and some quirky—albeit temporary— new sidekicks, and things get complicated. With every new development, Gabby prays that her "mucky streak" will end and the future will become clear. Yet every answer she uncovers leads her closer to danger—both for her life and for her heart.

Foul Play (**Book 8**)

Gabby St. Claire is crying "foul play" in every sense of the phrase. When the crime-scene cleaner agrees to go undercover at a local community theater, she discovers more than backstage bickering, atrocious acting, and rotten writing. The female lead is dead, and an old classmate who has staked everything on the musical production's success is about to go under. In her dual role of investigator and star of the show, Gabby finds the stakes rising faster than the opening-night curtain. She must face her past and make monumental decisions, not just about the play but also concerning her future relationships and career. Will Gabby find the killer before the curtain goes down—not only on the play, but also on life as she knows it?

Broom and Gloom (Book 9)

Gabby St. Claire is determined to get back in the saddle again. While in Oklahoma for a forensic conference, she meets her soon-to-be stepbrother, Trace Ryan, an up-and-coming country singer. A woman he was dating has disappeared, and he suspects a crazy fan may be behind it. Gabby agrees to investigate, as she tries to juggle her conference, navigate being alone in a new place, and locate a woman who may not want to be found. She discovers that sometimes taking life by the horns means staring danger in the face, no matter the consequences.

Dust and Obey (Book 10)

When Gabby St. Claire's ex-fiancé, Riley Thomas, asks for her help in investigating a possible murder at a couples retreat, she knows she should say no. She knows she should run far, far away from the danger of both being around Riley and the crime. But her nosy instincts and determination take precedence over her logic. Gabby and Riley must work together to find the killer. In the process, they have to confront demons from their past and deal with their present relationship.

Thrill Squeaker (**Book 11**)

An abandoned theme park. An unsolved murder. A decision that will change Gabby's life forever. Restoring an old amusement park and turning it into a destination resort seems like a fun idea for former crime-scene cleaner Gabby St. Claire. The side job gives her the chance to spend time with her friends, something she's missed since beginning a new career. The job turns out to be more than Gabby bargained for when she finds a dead body on her first day. Add to the mix legends of Bigfoot, creepy clowns, and ghostlike remnants of happier times at the park, and her stay begins to feel like a rollercoaster ride. Someone doesn't want the decrepit Mythical Falls to open again, but just how far is this person willing to go to ensure this venture fails? As the stakes rise and danger creeps closer, will Gabby be able to restore things in her own life that time has destroyed —including broken relationships? Or is her future closer to the fate of the doomed Mythical Falls?

Swept Away, **a Honeymoon Novella (Book 11.5)**

Finding the perfect place for a honeymoon, away from any potential danger or mystery, is challenging. But Gabby's longtime love and newly minted husband, Riley Thomas, has done it. He has found a location with a nonexistent crime rate, a mostly retired population, and plenty of opportunities for relaxation in the warm sun. Within minutes of the newlyweds' arrival, a convoy of vehicles pulls up to a nearby house, and their honeymoon oasis is destroyed like a sandcastle in a storm. Despite Gabby's and Riley's determination to keep to themselves, trouble comes knocking at their door—literally—when a neighbor is abducted from the beach directly outside their rental. Will Gabby and Riley be swept away with each other during their honeymoon . . . or will a tide of danger and mayhem pull them under?

Cunning Attractions (**Book 12**)

Politics. Love. Murder. Radio talk show host Bill McCormick is in his prime. He's dating a supermodel, his book is a bestseller, and his ratings have skyrocketed during the heated election season. But when Bill's ex-wife, Emma Jean, turns up dead, the media and his detractors assume the opinionated loudmouth is guilty of her murder. Bill's on-air rants about his demon-possessed ex don't help his case. Did someone realize that Bill was the perfect scapegoat? Or could Bill have silenced his Ice Queen ex once and for all? As Gabby comes closer to casting her vote for the guilty party, the stakes rise, tensions heat, and her own life is endangered. Will she be able to do a recount as votes are cast about who the murderer is? Or was this whole crime rigged from the start?

Clean Getaway (Book 13)

Gabby St. Claire Thomas has been given the opportunity of a lifetime: heading up a privately funded Cold Case Squad and handpicking the team members. Persnickety Evie Manson and nerdy Sherman Gilbert join forces with Gabby to bring justice and solace to families still wanting answers. On their first case, the Squad discovers that the murders of Ron and Margie Simmons are more than cold—they're frozen solid. The couple's anniversary celebration ended as a double homicide, and ten years later their daughter is still waiting for answers. But who would want to kill the loving couple? What kind of secrets were hiding beneath their cheery, All American exteriors? With every new lead, someone tries to sabotage their investigation . . . but the team might just end up being their own worst enemies. As a deadline presses in, can Gabby and her Squad bring the heat? Or will this cold-case killer make a clean getaway?

While You Were Sweeping, a **Riley Thomas Novella**

Riley Thomas is trying to come to terms with life after a traumatic brain injury turned his world upside down. Away from everything familiar—including his crime-scene-cleaning former fiancée and his career as a social-rights attorney—he's determined to prove himself and regain his old life. But when he claims he witnessed his neighbor shoot and kill someone, everyone thinks he's crazy. When all evidence of the crime disappears, even Riley has to wonder if he's losing his mind.

Note: *While You Were Sweeping* is a spin-off mystery written in conjunction with the Squeaky Clean series featuring crime-scene cleaner Gabby St. Claire.

Holly Anna Paladin Mysteries:

_____

Random Acts of Murder (**Book 1**)

When Holly Anna Paladin is given a year to live, she embraces her final days doing what she loves most—random acts of kindness. But one of her extreme good deeds goes horribly wrong, implicating her in a string of murders. Holly is suddenly thrust into a different kind of fight for her life. Could it also be random that the detective assigned to the case is her old high school crush and present-day nemesis? Will Holly find the killer before he ruins what is left of her life? Or will she spend her final days alone and behind bars?

Random Acts of Deceit (**Book 2**)

"Break up with Chase Dexter, or I'll kill him." Holly Anna Paladin never expected such a gut-wrenching ultimatum. With home invasions, hidden cameras, and bomb threats, Holly must make some serious choices. Whatever she decides, the consequences will either break her heart or break her soul. She tries to match wits with the Shadow Man, but the more she fights, the deeper she's drawn into the perilous situation. With her sister's wedding problems and the riots in the city, Holly has nearly reached her breaking point. She must stop this mystery man before someone she loves dies. But the deceit is threatening to pull her under . . . six feet under.

Random Acts of Malice (Book 3)

When Holly Anna Paladin's boyfriend, police detective Chase Dexter, says he's leaving for two weeks and can't give any details, she wants to trust him. But when she discovers Chase may be involved in some unwise and dangerous pursuits, she's compelled to intervene. Holly gets a run for her money as she's swept into the world of horseracing. The stakes turn deadly when a dead body surfaces and suspicion is cast on Chase. At every turn, more trouble emerges, making Holly question what she holds true about her relationship and her future. Just when she thinks she's on the homestretch, a dark horse arises. Holly might lose everything in a nail-biting fight to the finish.

Random Acts of Scrooge (Book 3.5)

Christmas is supposed to be the most wonderful time of the year, but a real-life Scrooge is threatening to ruin the season's good will. Holly Anna Paladin can't wait to celebrate Christmas with family and friends. She loves everything about the season—celebrating the birth of Jesus, singing carols, and baking Christmas treats, just to name a few. But when a local family needs help, how can she say no? Holly's community has come together to help raise funds to save the home of Greg and Babette Sullivan, but a Bah-Humburgler has snatched the canisters of cash. Holly and her boyfriend, police detective Chase Dexter, team up to catch the Christmas crook. Will they succeed in collecting enough cash to cover the Sullivans' overdue bills? Or will someone succeed in ruining Christmas for all those involved?

Random Acts of Greed (Book 4)

Help me. Don't trust anyone. Do-gooder Holly Anna Paladin can't believe her eyes when a healthy baby boy is left on her doorstep. What seems like good fortune quickly turns into concern when blood spatter is found on the bottom of the baby carrier. Something tragic— maybe deadly—happened in connection with the infant. The note left only adds to the confusion. What does it mean by "Don't trust anyone"? Holly is determined to figure out the identity of the baby. Is his mom someone from the inner-city youth center where she volunteers? Or maybe the connection is through Holly's former job as a social worker? Even worse—what if the blood belongs to the baby's mom? Every answer Holly uncovers only leads to more questions. A sticky web of intrigue captures her imagination until she's sure of only one thing: she must protect the baby at all cost.

Random Acts of Fraud (Book 5)

Vintage-loving Holly Anna Paladin finds online dating uncouth and unbecoming. But, in an attempt to overcome her romantic slump, her BFF convinces Holly to give it a shot. When Holly is stood up on her first date, she's halfway relieved . . . until she discovers the reason isn't because her cyber matchup has cold feet. Instead she stumbles upon him in a classic Mustang, deader than good old-fashioned manners. Holly's had enough with investigating crime and leaves her ex-boyfriend, Detective Chase Dexter, to solve this mystery. But Holly is somehow connected to this murder, and someone is determined to keep her in the thick of things. She hopes it's not Drew Williams, the handsome funeral director who's trying to sweep her off her feet. Before more people are hurt, Holly is determined to unmask the pretender in her life. But can she keep her feelings for Chase locked away? Or will Holly end up losing her heart to him all over again? She must solve the case before someone pulls the plug on her profile . . . and deletes her permanently.

The Sierra Files:

_____

Pounced (Book 1)

Animal-rights activist Sierra Nakamura never expected to stumble upon the dead body of a coworker while filming a project nor get involved in the investigation. But when someone threatens to kill her cats unless she hands over the "information," she becomes more bristly than an angry feline. Making matters worse is the fact that her cats—and the investigation—are driving a wedge between her and her boyfriend, Chad. With every answer she uncovers, old hurts rise to the surface and test her beliefs. Saving her cats might mean ruining everything else in her life. In the fight for survival, one thing is certain: either pounce or be pounced.

Hunted (Book 2)

Who knew a stray dog could cause so much trouble? Newlywed animal-rights activist Sierra Nakamura Davis must face her worst nightmare: breaking the news she eloped with Chad to her ultra-opinionated tiger mom. Her perfectionist parents have planned a vow-renewal ceremony at Sierra's lush childhood home, but a neighborhood dog ruins the rehearsal dinner when it shows up toting what appears to be a fresh human bone. While dealing with the dog, a nosy neighbor, and an old flame turning up at the wrong times, Sierra hunts for answers. Her journey of discovery leads to more than just who committed the crime.

Pranced (**Book 2.5, a Christmas novella**)

Sierra Nakamura Davis thinks spending Christmas with her husband's relatives will be a real Yuletide treat. But when the animal-rights activist learns his family has a reindeer farm, she begins to feel more like the Grinch. Even worse, when Sierra arrives, she discovers the reindeer are missing. Sierra fears the animals might be suffering a worse fate than being used for entertainment purposes. Can Sierra set aside her dogmatic opinions to help get the reindeer home in time for the holidays? Or will secrets tear the family apart and ruin Sierra's dream of the perfect Christmas?

Rattled (**Book 3**)

"What do you mean a thirteen-foot lavender albino ball python is missing?" Tough-as-nails Sierra Nakamura Davis isn't one to get flustered. But trying to balance being a wife and a new mom with her crusade to help animals is proving harder than she imagined. Add a missing

python, a high maintenance intern, and a dead body to the mix, and Sierra becomes the definition of rattled. Can she balance it all—and solve a possible murder—without losing her mind?

Carolina Moon Series:
_____

Home Before Dark (Book 1)

Nothing good ever happens after dark. Country singer Daleigh McDermott's father often repeated those words. Now, her father is dead. As she's about to flee back to Nashville, she finds his hidden journal with hints that his death was no accident. Mechanic Ryan Shields is the only one who seems to believe Daleigh. Her father trusted the man, but her attraction to Ryan scares her. She knows her life and career are back in Nashville and her time in the sleepy North Carolina town is only temporary. As Daleigh and Ryan work to unravel the mystery, it becomes obvious that someone wants them dead. They must rely on each other—and on God—if they hope to make it home before the darkness swallows them.

Gone By Dark (Book 2)

Ten years ago, Charity White's best friend, Andrea, was abducted as they walked home from school. A decade later, when Charity receives a mysterious letter that promises answers, she returns to North Carolina in search of closure. With the help of her new neighbor, Police Officer Joshua Haven, Charity begins to track down mysterious clues concerning her friend's abduction. They soon discover that they must work together or both of them will be swallowed by the looming darkness.

Wait Until Dark (Book 3)

Antiquarian Felicity French has no clue the trouble she's inviting in when she rescues a man outside her grandma's old plantation house during a treacherous snowstorm. Now she's stuck inside with a stranger sporting an old bullet wound and forgotten hours. Coast Guardsman Brody Joyner can't remember why he was out in such perilous weather, how he injured his head, or how a strange key got into his pocket. He also has no idea why his pint-sized savior has such a huge chip on her shoulder. He has no choice but to make the best of things until the storm passes. Brody and Felicity's rocky start goes from tense to worse when danger closes in. Who else wants the mysterious key that somehow ended up in Brody's pocket? Why? The unlikely duo quickly becomes entrenched in an adventure of a lifetime, one that could have ties to local folklore and Felicity's ancestors. But sometimes the past leads to darkness . . . darkness that doesn't wait for anyone.

Light the Dark (a Christmas novella)

Nine months pregnant, Hope Solomon is on the run and fearing for her life. Desperate for warmth, food, and shelter, she finds what looks like an abandoned house. Inside, she discovers a Christmas that's been left behind —complete with faded decorations on a brittle Christmas tree and dusty stockings filled with loss. Someone spies smoke coming from the chimney of the empty house and alerts Dr. Luke Griffin, the owner. He rarely visits the home that harbors so many bittersweet memories for him. Then Luke meets Hope, and he knows this mother-to-be desperately needs help. With no room at any local inn, Luke invites Hope to stay, unaware of the danger following her. While running from the darkness, the embers of Christmas present are stirred with an unexpected birth and a holiday romance. But will Hope and Luke live to see a Christmas future?

Taken by Dark

Widowed single mom Willa Summers can't deny that something strange is going on in her North Carolina hometown. She fears her pregnant sister-in-law, singer Daleigh McDermott, is the target of myste- rious threats. Little does Willa know that she's the one in danger. When Declan Donovan shows up in the house next door, things seem to turn from bad to worse. Declan broke Willa's heart more than a decade ago when he deserted her and chose a career with the FBI over small-town life with her. But now he may be the only one who can help keep everyone safe. Declan must get to the bottom of things before the mysterious threats become reality. As the dark closes in, everything Willa holds dear may be snatched from her—including a second chance at love. Will she be overtaken by the dark or will she escape its clutches in time?

Cape Thomas Series:
_____

Dubiosity (Book 1)

Savannah Harris vowed to leave behind her old life as an investigative reporter. But when two migrant workers go missing, her curiosity spikes. As more eerie incidents begin afflicting the area, each works to draw Savannah out of her seclusion and raise the stakes—for her and the surrounding community. Even as Savannah's new boarder, Clive Miller, makes her feel things she thought long forgotten, she suspects he's hiding something too, and he's not the only one. As secrets emerge and danger closes in, Savannah must choose between faith and uncertainty. One wrong decision might spell the end . . . not just for her but for everyone around her. Will she unravel the mystery in time, or will doubt get the best of her?

Disillusioned (Book 2)

Nikki Wright is desperate to help her brother, Bobby, who hasn't been the same since escaping from a detainment camp run by terrorists in Colombia. Rumor has it that he betrayed his navy brothers and conspired with those who held him hostage, and both the press and the military are hounding him for answers. All Nikki wants is to shield her brother so he has time to recover and heal. But soon they realize the paparazzi are the least of their worries. When a group of men try to abduct Nikki and her brother, Bobby insists that Kade Wheaton, another former SEAL, can keep them out of harm's way. But can Nikki trust Kade? After all, the man who broke her heart eight years ago is anything but safe... Hiding out in a farmhouse on the Chesapeake Bay, Nikki finds her loyalties—and the remnants of her long-held faith—tested as she and Kade put aside their differences to keep Bobby's increasingly erratic behavior under wraps. But when Bobby disappears, Nikki will have to trust Kade completely if she wants to uncover the truth about a rumored conspiracy. Nikki's life—and the fate of the nation—depends on it.

Distorted (**Book 3**)

Mallory Baldwin is a survivor. A former victim of human trafficking, she's been given a second chance, yet not a night goes by that she doesn't remember being a slave to weapons dealer Dante Torres. Despite being afraid of the dark and wary of strangers, Mallory is trying to rebuild her life by turning her tragedy into redemption. To former Navy SEAL Tennyson Walker, Mallory seems nothing like the shattered woman he rescued two years ago, and he can't help but be inspired by her strength and resilience. So when a stalker suddenly makes Mallory vulnerable once again,

Tennyson steps up as her bodyguard to keep her safe. Mallory and Tennyson's mutual attraction can't be ignored, but neither can Mallory's suspicion that Tennyson is keeping a terrible secret about her past. As the nightmare closes in, it's not only Mallory and Tennyson's love that comes under fire but their very lives as well. Will their faith sustain them? Or will the darkness win once and for all?

The Good Girl

Tara Lancaster can sing "Amazing Grace" in three harmonies, two languages, and interpret it for the hearing impaired. She can list the Bible canon backward, forward, and alphabetized. The only time she ever missed church was when she had pneumonia and her mom made her stay home. Then her life shatters and her reputation is left in ruins. She flees halfway across the country to dog-sit, but the quiet anonymity she needs isn't waiting at her sister's house. Instead, she finds a knife with a threatening message, a fame-hungry friend, a too-hunky neighbor, and evidence of . . . a ghost? Following all the rules has gotten her nowhere. And nothing she learned in Sunday School can tell her where to go from there.

Death of the Couch Potato's Wife (**Suburban Sleuth Mysteries**)

You haven't seen desperate until you've met Laura

Berry, a career-oriented city slicker turned suburbanite housewife. Well-trained in the big-city commandment, "mind your own business," Laura is persuaded by her spunky seventy-year-old neighbor, Babe, to check on another neighbor who hasn't been seen in days. She finds Candace Flynn, wife of the infamous "Couch King," dead, and at last has a reason to get up in the morning. Someone is determined to stop her from digging deeper into the death of her neighbor, but Laura is just as determined to figure out who is behind the death-by-poisoned-pork-rinds.

Imperfect

Since the death of her fiancé two years ago, novelist Morgan Blake's life has been in a holding pattern. She has a major case of writer's block, and a book signing in the mountain town of Perfect sounds as perfect as its name. Her trip takes a wrong turn when she's involved in a hit-and-run: She hit a man, and he ran from the scene. Before fleeing, he mouthed the word "Help." First she must find him. In Perfect, she finds a small town that offers all she ever wanted. But is something sinister going on behind its cheery exterior? Was she invited as a guest of honor simply to do a book signing? Or was she lured to town for another purpose—a deadly purpose?

The Gabby St. Claire Diaries:

A TWEEN MYSTERY SERIES

The Curtain Call Caper (Book 1)

Is a ghost haunting the Oceanside Middle School auditorium? What else could explain the disasters surrounding the play—everything from missing scripts to a falling spotlight and damaged props? Seventh-grader Gabby St. Claire has dreamed about being part of her school's musical, but a series of unfortunate events threatens to shut down the production. While trying to uncover the culprit and save her fifteen minutes of fame, she also has to manage impossible teachers, cliques, her dysfunctional family, and a secret she can't tell even her best friend. Will Gabby figure out who or what is sabotaging the show . . . or will it be curtains for her and the rest of the cast?

The Disappearing Dog Dilemma (Book 2)

Why are dogs disappearing around town? When two friends ask seventh-grader Gabby St. Claire for her help in finding their missing canines, Gabby decides to unleash her sleuthing skills to sniff out whoever is behind the act. But time management and relationships get tricky as worrisome weather, a part-time job, and a new crush interfere with Gabby's investigation. Will her determination crack the case? Or will shadowy villains, a penchant for overcommitting, and even her own heart put her in the doghouse?

The Bungled Bike Burglaries (**Book 3**)

Stolen bikes and a long-forgotten time capsule leave one amateur sleuth baffled and busy. Seventh-grader Gabby St. Claire is determined to bring a bike burglar to justice—and not just because mean girl Donabell Bullock is strong-arming her. But each new clue brings its own set of trouble. As if that's not enough, Gabby finds evidence of a decades-old murder within the contents of the time capsule, but no one seems to take her seriously. As her investigation heats up, will Gabby's knack for being in the wrong place at the wrong time with the wrong people crack the case? Or will it prove hazardous to her health?

About the Author

USA Today has called Christy Barritt's books "scary, funny, passionate, and quirky."

Christy writes both mystery and romantic suspense novels that are clean with underlying messages of faith. Her books have won the Daphne du Maurier Award for Excellence in Suspense and Mystery, have been twice nominated for the Romantic Times Reviewers' Choice Award, and have finaled for both a Carol Award and Foreword Magazine's Book of the Year.

She is married to her Prince Charming, a man who thinks she's hilarious—but only when she's not trying to be. Christy is a self-proclaimed klutz, an avid music lover who's known for spontaneously bursting into song, and a road trip aficionado.

When she's not working or spending time with her family, she enjoys singing, playing the guitar, and exploring small, unsuspecting towns where people have no idea how accident-prone she is.

Find Christy online at:
   www.christybarritt.com
   www.facebook.com/christybarritt
   www.twitter.com/cbarritt

Sign up for Christy's newsletter to get information on all
of   her   latest   releases   here:
www.christybarritt.com/newsletter-sign-up/

**If you enjoyed this book, please consider
leaving a review.**

Made in the USA
Monee, IL
30 September 2021

79034207R00184